The world according to Harry Rice:

....

Intuition—"I read mail better than I read people."
Common Sense—"When a situation calls for common
    sense, I sometimes have a tendency to employ
    moronic logic."
The Cure for What Ails You—"Whenever my idea of
    humanity begins to decompose or I need to get
    my dignity out of hock, I go to the beach."
Lawyers—"There's a common misconception that
    Hispanics are the majority population group
    in South Florida. Not so. It's lawyers."
Life's Little Mysteries—"Too often I find myself
    asking, how come everybody knows that but
    me?"

• • •

"Not a bad place to spend a couple of hours with
    a cool drink on a hot, sunny day."
        —*The Drood Review of Mystery*

· · · The · · ·
HARRY
Chronicles

Allan Pedrazas

HarperPaperbacks
A Division of HarperCollinsPublishers

HarperPaperbacks
A Division of HarperCollins*Publishers*
10 East 53rd Street, New York, N.Y. 10022-5299

This is a work of fiction. The characters, incidents, and
dialogues are products of the author's imagination and are not to
be construed as real. Any resemblance to actual events or
persons, living or dead, is entirely coincidental.

ISBN 0-06-104435-0

Cover illustration by Raul Colon

A hardcover edition of this book was published in 1995 by
St. Martin's Press.

First HarperPaperbacks printing: March 1997

Printed in the United States of America

Visit HarperPaperbacks on the World Wide Web at
http://www.harpercollins.com/paperbacks

10 9 8 7 6 5 4 3 2 1

For Doris

··· The ···
HARRY
Chronicles

one

•••••

The man who hated dwarfs was sitting at the end of the bar whispering his sins to Father Shifty. It was confessional hour at the Sand Bar, which is just about all the time, inasmuch as sin on the beach is as plentiful as the shells. Father Shifty appeared to be more disconcerted by the empty glass in front of him than by the confessor's transgressions. Absolution could be had for the price of another round. Penance on the rocks.

The Sand Bar is Father Shifty's favorite place of worship when Carla Meadows is working. Admittedly, as a bartender Carla is more adept at pampering wayward clergy and lost souls than I am.

Father Shifty comes from a large Irish family. During his childhood he was tithed to the church as the family's designated emissary to God. It seems that in those days all large Irish families spawned at least one priest, if not a nun. Father Shifty was sent to the seminary in search of an answer, though he wasn't quite sure of the question. His teachers said he lacked discipline and had a short attention span, which Father Shifty claimed was a prerequisite to sitting through any meeting with a monsignor or a parish fund-raiser. During the sixties the young priest became a "radical pacifist, the chic minority of the decade." His words. He was a casualty of a televised anti-war demonstration. "A pep rally for peace." Unfortunately, a Vatican warlord saw Father Shifty's on-camera interview. The militant priest was documented on film, criticizing the Catholic Church for its repressive dogma and for peddling ecumenical illusions. Father Shifty also accused the Church of failing the free-spirited youth of America. "Ironic, since the Church was founded on the revolutionary teachings of Christ." It was bad enough that Father Shifty had grouped Jesus with Abbie Hoffman and Jerry Rubin, two Jewish Yippies. But he crossed the line when he referred to Pope John XXIII as "Little Caesar." The church stripped Father Shifty of everything but his moral convictions.

Father Shifty was the holiest man I knew. He could set up shop in the Sand Bar anytime as far as I was concerned.

I was sitting several stools down from the public confessional, scanning the classifieds for a free cat.

Behind the bar, Carla was slicing limes, peeling lemons, setting up for the day. Overhead, a paddle fan circulated the sweet, salt-water-scented air floating in off the Atlantic. Not the inane pace of the city, nor the canned atmosphere of a glass high-rise, but those are the sacrifices you make when doing business on the beach.

It was a weekday morning, too early for most tourists to sit at a bar, nursing a beer. Typically, they spent mornings supine on the sand giving their hundred-dollar-a-day tans a workout in the sizzling sun. Proof they had gotten their money's worth on their Florida vacation. The usual Sand Bar cast of characters was at work pumping gas, waiting tables in restaurants, baiting hooks on charter boats, renting bicycles, booking reservations, selling beachwear, tattooing nubile behinds, or performing other assorted tourist-industry-related services. It's what the residents do in coastal towns.

The man who hated dwarfs stood up to leave. He mumbled something.

Father Shifty nodded dutifully. "Don't forget, Jesus loves you."

"If Jesus loves me, then why is the stock market down?" said the man who hated dwarfs. He walked out.

Father Shifty called after him, "I didn't say He loved you a lot." He shook his head lethargically and muttered, " 'Tis a strange way to make a living."

"How's that?" I said, still thumbing through the classifieds.

He glanced down the expanse of bar at me. "People insist on telling me things I don't want to know. Why do you suppose that is, Harry?"

"Maybe it's your act," I said, not looking up from the newspaper.

"No." He slapped the bar. "I'll tell you what it is. It's the curse of the righteous misfits."

I looked over at him. "You ever notice you only ask questions you know the answers to?"

Father Shifty pondered that charge for a moment. "Why do you suppose that is?"

I laughed. "I don't know, but I'm sure you do."

He stared at me for a few seconds. "It's because I'm a wise man," he concluded.

"You should be listed in the yellow pages."

"Are you listening to this sacrilege, Carla? Do you hear how your jaded employer mocks the once and future patron saint of flower power? You surely have been raised better than to treat a holy man irreverently."

Carla was at the sink, washing citrus juice from her hands. She grabbed a bar towel and started to dry off.

"Actually, Father, before you, I never had much exposure to any church or religion."

Father Shifty arched his caterpillar-size eyebrows. "You're Catholic, no?"

"Sort of. Italian Catholic," Carla said. "We believe that olive oil and garlic will cure whatever ails the body or spirit."

The fallen priest smiled. "And the Irish will tell you there's nothing like a good mea culpa and a shot of rotgut to cleanse the soul."

"Whatever happened to silent prayer?" I said.

"That's reserved for football games and holy wars."

At that moment the door opened. A man came in. The first thing I noticed about him was that he was tall. He had probably played college basketball twenty years ago. He had a rich man's tan and a salon-styled do. He stood in the doorway, looking around. A definite first-timer. A bar regular walks in as if he's at home. The man wore sunglasses shaped like a Ferrari windshield, a navy blazer, a burgundy silk tie, a white shirt, gray slacks, and soft leather loafers. Dressed for success. He was the embodiment of the kind of man who *reads Playboy*.

Though he was dressed assuredly, his manner was uncertain as he approached the bar. He did not sit.

Carla greeted him and asked if she could help.

"I'm not sure," he said. He looked doubtfully at Father Shifty, at me, and again at Carla. "I think this is the right address. I was told I could find Harry Rice here."

Carla gestured with her head. "That's Harry over there."

The man regarded me skeptically. "You?"

I nodded.

"You're Harry Rice?"

I nodded again. I'm told I have a tendency to repeat myself.

He walked over and handed me his business card. I glanced at it. It said: WADE LOFTUS—ENTERTAINMENT & SPORTS LAW. There was also an address and phone number. I looked at Wade Loftus.

"Eloise Loftus is my wife." He said that as if it explained everything. He dipped his long fingers into the breast pocket of his blazer and drew out a fifty-dollar bill. He laid the money on the bar in front of me. "That's severance pay. Consider yourself fired." He started to walk out, stopped, turned back, and pointed a shaking finger at me. "And stay away from my wife." With that he left.

I could sense Carla's and Father Shifty's eyes on me.

"Harry, you old reprobate," Father Shifty said. "You surprise me. But you're in luck." He was rubbing his hands gleefully. "Adultery just happens to be my specialty."

Carla came over and stood across the bar from me. She was grinning as if she was delighted to have learned some dark secret about me. "Okay, Harry," she cooed. "What was that all about?"

I shrugged. "I think somebody dialed the wrong number."

"I don't know. He sure knew your name. So tell me, who is this Eloise Loftus?"

I pocketed the business card and the fifty dollars. "Carla, I have no idea. I've never heard of Eloise Loftus."

two

•••••

Eloise Loftus sat in the canvas director's chair beside my desk in the Sand Bar office. She sat properly, resting her hands atop the eel-skin briefcase on her lap. She was dressed properly: a high-collar blouse and a sea-blue serge suit that could not disguise breasts proportionately too large for her otherwise petite frame. She carried a proper purse, which probably contained a rather proper Mercedes-Benz key chain. She emanated a very proper image for one exuding a bordello sensuality. Maybe it was her sultry oval lips, which could probably talk me into anything. Or it could have been those mysterious eyes, a shade darker than sin. Whatever it was, she had all the ingredients. I've only seen it in middle-aged women, an indefinable quality that makes them appealing in a Jeanne Moreau sort of way. Not pretty, but deceivingly sexy. Take the parts separately, and nothing spectacular: legs too short, breasts bigger than the illusion requires, black hair cropped boyishly short, intimidating eyes, emasculating lips. Put it all together, though, and pass the apple.

I could not take my eyes off her.

She brushed a renegade strand of hair from her forehead and studied me with a steady gaze. "You know you're staring at me," she said with a faint smile.

"No, I am admiring you," I said. "It's a subtle difference, I'll grant you."

"Thank you. That's sweet."

I growled Norman Mailerly, "I don't do sweet."

"That's a shame. I think you'd be good at it," she replied smoothly. Then her tone abruptly changed to business. "I'm here, Mr. Rice, because it's my understanding that you are a private investigator."

"Sometimes."

"It's rather odd that you operate from a bar."

I wasn't sure if that was a question or an editorial, so I said, "It's a long story."

"I don't particularly care for long stories," she said casually. "Unfortunately, I do have an insatiable curiosity."

I leaned back in my chair. After a second's thought I opted to give her the abridged edition of "How It Was I Came to Be Who I Am." "Before I bought the Sand Bar my sole source of income was from private investigation. I didn't like being dependent on the whims of suspicious spouses. I got tired of chasing after teenage runaways. And spying on underpaid employees for stingy employers left a bad taste in my mouth. With the Sand Bar I can afford to be selective. I don't have to take every case that comes along."

"You're that good?"

"I'm that selective."

She considered that while she looked around the office. "Why do you still do it? Investigate, I mean."

"Breaks up the routine. And for the money. The bar is self-sustaining most of the time. But during the rainy season, and the ebbs between tourist seasons, beach businesses don't do very well."

She looked right at me. "Does that mean you're expensive?"

"It depends on the job. It depends on how much money I need and to some extent how much the market will bear."

"In other words, you're not expensive if the client can afford you."

"That's another way of putting it."

She appraised me with slightly amused eyes for a moment. Finally she said, "Well, if you don't need too much money, and if I can afford you, I think I'd like to hire you."

"Just like that?" She didn't strike me as the type to make snap decisions.

"No, not just like that. Actually, there are three reasons, but primarily because you were recommended by a colleague."

"Anyone I know?"

"Mali Addis."

The secret word. Mali Addis, best friend and former lover. During the two years that Mali and I were on again, off again friends and lovers in one, I could count on one hand the number of times that she did not talk about her former live-in. Mali was still carrying a torch for the jerk, who had dumped her years ago to play soldier of fortune in Yellowstone National Park. The coup de grace for us came one night over dinner. I had been talking about taking her to Europe to visit one of her girlfriends when Mali started talking about the Gucci watch Chuckie had bought her many years before. It was as if she hadn't heard a word I had said. It had a chilling effect on our physical relationship, but in a strange way it seemed to bond our friendship. I think what it was, was at that moment I realized that women didn't have any more of a clue about relationships than men did. They may talk about relationships more than men, but when it comes to understanding them, the sorority is as screwed up as the fraternity. What a relief it was to learn that I wasn't a solitary freak in a world of self-assured lovers who didn't know how confusing things really were.

"You teach English?" It was a natural assumption. Mali taught twentieth-century American poetry at the community college. It was one of many common interests Mali and I shared, though my knowledge of American poetry was severely limited to Charles Bukowski, Percy Dovetonsils, and the works of an anonymous men's-room poet.

"No. I'm an associate professor of humanities." She pronounced "humanities" like it was a form of adult entertainment. Taught properly, it just might be.

I sat through a pregnant pause, waiting to see if Eloise Loftus would volunteer what Mali had said about me in her recommendation. It didn't happen. For lack of anything better to say, I said: "You mentioned that there were three reasons why you wanted to hire me."

"Yes, I did," she said slowly, considering whether to tell me the others. "The second reason is, you're discreet. You haven't spoken of my husband's visit here this morning."

I nodded. "Wade Loftus, Entertainment and Sports Law. He tips well."

"So I heard."

"What else does he do?"

She shrugged. "Besides his law practice, he has half-interest in an apartment building in Pompano Beach. Tonight he'll be teaching a civics class at BCC. Tomorrow morning it's a Kiwanis breakfast."

"He keeps busy."

She didn't respond to that.

"What was the third reason?"

"That . . ." She paused, thought a moment, then shook her head. "That's my business. All that matters is I have decided to hire you."

"That's only half of what matters."

"Of course. You haven't accepted."

She had a quick mind.

"What would you like to know?" she said.

"Well, since you brought him up, how did your husband know about me before I knew about him?"

"I've been thinking about hiring a private detective for several weeks now. A few nights ago I was talking to Mali at a faculty cocktail party. I told her what I had been thinking and she gave me your name. Last night I told Wade I was planning to hire you. He threw one of his puerile tantrums. Obviously he wasn't listening. Somehow he construed that I had already hired you."

"And now he construes that I've been fired."

"Wade may construe whatever he likes. I'm more concerned with what you think, Mr. Rice. Are you hired or fired?"

I frowned, going for the pensive look.

She tilted her head and gazed at me. "Are you all right?" she asked.

My pensive look needed work. "I'm fine. Why don't you tell me just what it is you want me to do for you."

"About three months ago, the last week in June, our apartment was burglarized." She opened her briefcase and removed a legal-size manila folder. "This contains the insurance company's list of everything that was taken."

"From the size of that file it looks like everything was stolen."

"That's exactly right. The apartment was emptied of everything. It was as if we had moved out and left nothing behind. A copy of the police report is in there, too."

I looked through the file. There was an itemized list of all the stolen goods, along with the estimated values. Furniture, pictures, lamps, silverware, televisions, stereo equipment, clothes, kitchen appliances, an antique gun collection.

"You've received a check from the insurance company?" I asked as I flipped through the police report.

"Yes."

I looked at her. "But you feel the insurance company shortchanged you by a considerable amount."

Her eyebrows arched. She was impressed. I like that in a woman.

"It's simple, Mrs. Loftus. You would not be willing to pay an investigator's fee if there had been an equitable settlement. So I have to assume there is a significant difference of opinion, a lot of money at stake. Otherwise, you would be foolish to risk additional expense just for a chance of recovery." I glanced at the list again. "The guns?"

"Yes."

"What's the difference in your appraised value and the insurance company's?"

"Conservatively, the collection was worth a hundred thousand dollars. The insurance company said twenty-five thousand."

"That's quite a gap."

"Indeed."

"What about the rest of your property?"

"They were fair."

"A seventy-five-thousand-dollar difference, huh?"

"A seventy-five-thousand-dollar mistake."

Three months was a long time. Still, a concentrated effort, something the police would not have the time or resources or inclination for, might turn up a lead, especially on an antique gun collection. There were more than two dozen guns, some over a century old. With some connections I had, two weeks would be enough time, if the job could be done. After that it would be a waste of time.

"What is it you want back?" I asked. "Everything, or just the guns?"

"Everything would be nice, but not necessary. Most of the household has been replaced. I will settle for the gun collection."

It was time to find out if she could afford me. "Five thousand dollars, plus expenses, buys you two weeks. If I find the guns tomorrow it's still five thousand dollars. Also, I get a ten percent finder's bonus of the seventy-five-thousand-dollar difference upon recovery. Naturally, if I don't find all of the guns we'll prorate the bonus."

She sat there like she was waiting for me to come to my senses. Eventually she said, "If you're successful you want five thousand dollars plus ten percent of the recovery. If you're not successful I'm out five thousand dollars, plus expenses. Do I understand you correctly?"

"I believe you do."

Her dark eyes locked on mine. "Are you a gambler, Mr. Rice?"

"I've placed a few bets."

"All right then, here's my offer. Ten thousand dollars or nothing. You take as long as you want. Two days, two weeks, or two months. You recover the guns, you collect. If you don't find the collection, I don't pay." While I mulled that over she continued: "Or, I'll give you five thousand dollars for two weeks. No expenses. No bonus. A flat five thousand dollars whether you deliver or not."

"What if I recover only part of the collection?"

"Twenty-five percent of the recovered value, not to exceed ten thousand dollars."

So the question was, how much faith did I have in myself? Damn, I liked this woman. I liked her lips. What the hell, I'd worked for less persuasive reasons than that.

"All right, Mrs. Loftus. Ten thousand dollars. If I find nothing, you pay nothing."

"No advance, then."

"I understand that."

She offered her hand.

And that's how it started.

three

....

I did not become a private detective because of some calling. I'm not a crusader. Yes, I like to see a wrong corrected, but I don't thirst for revenge. I've accepted jobs I didn't want, simply because there was no one else who would do it. If that sounds noble, it shouldn't. I operate on the assumption that I'm going to be paid for my services. It doesn't always happen that way. I know that going in. So why do I do it?

There are stock answers I can give to that question. Answers that sound good. If the right person ever asked that question, I would have to tell the truth: I don't know. It's one of the mysteries I've not been inclined to solve. How did I end up doing this for a living? I think that's one of those questions most people avoid. Not that I'm complaining. I'm not. I'm better off than most people. I know that. I have my health. There are a few good people I can call friends. I can afford to do many of the things I want to do. Not everything, but there's nothing to whine about. If I could change a few things about me I would. I wish I had a closer relationship with my daughter. I would prefer it if there hadn't been so many women in my life. I would trade them all for that special one, that kindred spirit who has eluded me. My life has always worked better when it's been accompanied by female encouragement, female sensibility, and the emotional protein that the right woman always seems to radiate. Yeah, I'd lock on to that in a heartbeat. Commitment doesn't scare me. What does is committing to the wrong person. I did that once. I'd rather go it alone than make that mistake again.

That may be why I'm such a dazzling failure at judging character. I've become so cautious looking for things that aren't there that I'm not seeing what's in front of me. I have to keep reminding myself of that. And that's what I was thinking about as I watched Eloise Loftus walk out of my office. My mind was Ping-Pong-ing back and forth between Go for it and Run for your life. It really didn't matter whether she was different from all other women or the same as all other women. Because I never know the difference until it's too late.

Recognizing a problem is not the same as solving it.

• • •

I spent the rest of the afternoon at Cuban Frankie's, huddled over a plate of black beans, rice, chopped onions, marinated *palomilla* steak, and fried plantains, and the manila folder that Eloise Loftus had left with me. I sat at a Formica-top table by the window so I could read the police report. The lighting in Cuban Frankie's is reminiscent of a smoky, nocturnal coffeehouse of the fifties, where pale women with long straight hair and names like Honey and Sparrow gave poetry readings. In the far corner of Cuban Frankie's, in a red Naugahyde booth, two ancient men sat drinking espresso from pill-size cups. They played dominoes and carried on a muted dialogue in Spanish. I imagined that like most old Cubans, they

were plotting the day they would hit the beach and recapture their motherland from Castro.

The kitchen door swung open. The waitress came out,
carrying two bottles of beer. I watched as she walked
across the warped linoleum floor. She stopped at my table
and eased into the chair across from me. She pushed one
of the bottles toward me. "Have a beer with me, Harry?"

"All right, Connie, but you'll owe me a favor." I took
the beer. "What's the occasion?"

She shrugged. "My birthday."

We touched bottles in a toast. "Should I send a card?"
I said.

"No. Just leave a massive tip."

"Done deal."

We drank. I kept my eyes on Connie. She was staring
out the window at nothing in particular. She was medi-
tatively quiet. I had the feeling she wanted more than a
drinking buddy.

"Birthday blues?" I said.

"No. Jesus, no." She smiled sweetly. "Not me, Harry.
I shoved that age-and-death stuff in the closet years ago
when my breasts started to sag. Growing old doesn't
bother me. Actually, I like getting older, getting straight,
getting truer perspectives. It's the only way to go. Let's
face it, youth wasn't so hot. In fact, it was a joke." She
stared out the window, then slowly shook her head. "You
know what the world needs, Harry? Magic. All the magic
is gone."

"It's still there, Connie. It's just not a twenty-four-
hour-a-day, every day, ride. If it was we'd all be coasting
along in a sea of beauty, brimming with belly laughs.
And if we were all doing that, all the time, there'd be
nothing magical about it."

Connie shifted in her chair. "That sounds like Eastern
religion mystic bullshit. The Great Magician in the Sky

doles out magic tricks sparingly to every good boy and girl. Give me a break, Harry."

I grinned sheepishly. "Well, what did you expect? If you want a massive tip you've got to listen to my nonsense."

"The tip hasn't been born that's worth listening to you philosophize for." She glanced at her watch. "I've got to start getting set up for the dinner crowd." Connie got out of her seat. She leaned across the table and kissed me on top of the head. "Thanks, Harry. You've a gift that few men have."

"That's what all the biker babes tell me."

Connie slapped me playfully on the shoulder. "Asshole. That's not what I'm talking about. You know how to listen."

"Ah, get out of here. Leave me alone. My black beans are getting cold."

I had to agree with Connie about one thing. Magic. It was going to take a heap of magic for me to find that antique gun collection. After reading the police report, I was almost convinced that only a magician could have stolen the Loftus household effects. Only sorcery could explain how someone could have slipped the entire contents of an apartment through a locked and bolted door, down a hallway and elevator, out to the parking lot, and onto a truck in broad daylight without anyone seeing a thing.

According to the police report, on the morning of June 28, at 0800, Wade Loftus left the Hallandale Beach condominium for work. He returned that evening at approximately 1830 to find the apartment stripped clean. He immediately phoned the police department from the building's lobby. Officers Alfredo Vidaurri and Strut Sumner responded to the call and arrived on the scene at 1850. Despite the presence of a dead bolt lock on the apartment door, there was no sign of forced entry. The sliding glass doors leading to the fourth-story balcony were still locked from the inside and had not been tampered with. Besides Wade and Eloise Loftus, only the building manager had a key to the apartment.

Wade Loftus told the officers he was running late that morning and may have left the door unlocked out of habit. Since he usually left the apartment first in the morning, his wife would lock up when she left for work. However, that week Eloise Loftus was in Gainesville taking care of her cousin's daughter while the girl's mother was in the hospital recovering from surgery.

Officers Vidaurri and Sumner canvassed the building. Of those spoken to, no one had seen anything, and none had been home for the whole day. There was no single time span, though, when everyone was out.

There was one entry on the security guard's incident log for that day. At approximately 1530 hours, the complex's security guard was called to the fourth floor by Lynn Robinette, who lives in the apartment directly across the hall from the Loftus apartment. Robinette reported several teenage boys roaming the corridor—boys who did not live in the adults-only condo. The security guard chased the boys out of the building and then went back and checked every apartment on the fourth floor. Where the residents were not home, the guard tested the doorknobs to make sure the apartments were locked. All the vacant apartments were locked, including 409, the Loftus apartment. No one reported anything missing. Until Wade Loftus returned home that evening.

• • •

It was nearly dusk by the time I walked back into the Sand Bar. At one of the tables a displaced Hawaiian shirt, stuffed with a Marlboro-smoking tourist, was hunched over a Florida guidebook. Slumped on a stool at the near end of the bar was a regular, a mate on a charter fishing yacht. There were two piles of bills on the bar in front of him. It was a biweekly ritual. He would cash his check and divide the money. The larger stack was for child support; the little pile was for rent or binge-drinking. The mate was choking a long-neck of beer. He was mumbling something about love being a fad. Too often, bars sub for psychiatric wards and the patrons become more patients than customers.

Nick Triandos, the evening bartender, had relieved Carla. He was drawing draft beers at the far end of the bar for Al and Irma. They ran Al's Bike Rentals next door.

Al saw me and waved me over. "Sit down, Harry. I'll buy you a beer."

It was a little game we played. Al would buy me a beer and then I'd buy them two. That's the kind of bar it is.

"I could use one," I said, climbing onto the stool next to Irma. I leaned over and whispered, "Hi, sexy." Then I nibbled on her earlobe.

Irma squirmed. "Ohhh, Harry. It's lucky for Al I'm not into younger men."

"Shit," Al mumbled. "It's lucky for younger men. Nick, this better be my last beer. Irma's beginning to look good."

"Irma," I said, "don't let him talk to you like that."

"What's a girl to do?" She sighed mockingly. "He's my cross."

"Why'd you ever marry him?"

She shrugged. "There was nothing good on television that night."

Al yelped, "I don't believe this woman! I've let her follow me across seven state lines. I've taught her the bike rental business. I buy her new dish sponges every

Christmas. I've taken her to most of the VFW dances. I've given her two sons, raised them, schooled them, locked them out. She's got three grandchildren to comfort her in her old age that she wouldn't have had if it wasn't for me. I've loved her thin. I've loved her not thin. I've made her home the envy of the Women's Club. Thirty-seven years I've devoted to making her the happiest woman alive. Does she appreciate it? Hell, Harry, she still hasn't told her mother about me."

Irma shook, laughing. "I've been such a fool."

"Damn right."

"I better take you home and give you some nourishment, Al. I think you're running a quart low. Join us for dinner, Harry?"

"Rain check," I said. "I'm going to turn in early tonight. I've got a full day tomorrow. Started a new case today."

Irma helped Al off the bar stool. As she pulled him toward the door, Al turned back and called to me, "Don't forget, I bought the last round."

I watched Al and Irma walk out, holding hands like high-school sweethearts.

Nick Triandos listened silently as I told him about Eloise and Wade Loftus and their gun collection. Nick did everything quietly. Usually, his half of a conversation was limited to facial expressions. Nick was the size of a plow horse, but for a retired noncommissioned officer his reflexes were still as quick as a good Triple-A fastball, though his legs were as heavy as a third-string catcher's. A black-and-gray crew cut outlined his weathered olive face. With a walrus mustache, Nick looked like a Greek Hoss Cartwright.

"Not so smart," he said, when I told him about the all-or-nothing contingency fee.

"I'm beginning to think so myself," I admitted.

It was dark out. I was in a lazy mood. No more detecting for the day. Tomorrow morning I would start asking a lot of questions. Like, was the dead bolt locked when Wade Loftus came home that night? If it was, somebody had to have a key. So who knew the Loftus home would be empty? Who else could have had a key? Who knew Eloise Loftus was out of town? Who knew about the gun collection? Had anyone tried to buy it? Was the gun collection the target of the thieves, or was it incidental? The police report said, "of those spoken to"— did that mean they hadn't spoken to everyone? They must have missed someone. There would have been too much activity to go unnoticed. A moving van? Movers in the hall? I needed to talk to Wade Loftus. I needed to see Eloise Loftus. See the condo manager about his key security. Recanvass the tenants. See Sam Maturano about the guns. Then what?

It could wait till tomorrow. Some of the evening regulars were beginning to drift in. I decided to hang around for a while, play some liar's poker, offer sage advice, and agree with everyone about anything, so they could believe what they needed to believe. I ordered a pitcher of beer.

It was too early to turn in early.

four

......

There's a common misconception that Hispanics are the majority population group in South Florida. Not so. It's lawyers.

It was inevitable, as southern Florida was transformed from a tropical paradise into a septic tank of greed, overflowing with drug dealers, bankers, rent-a-murderers, developers, deep-pocketed building inspectors, convicted-felon politicians, child pornographers, real estate agents, muggers, no-return-address accountants, loan sharks, hoods, pimps, hookers, judges for sale, witnesses for hire, burglars, car thieves, small-time hustlers, grifters, mendacious clergymen, retired "Sue the bastards" New Yorkers, con men, alleged rehabilitated recidivists, and doctors with the scruples of used-car salesmen. The stench was bound to attract a horde of predatory shysters to the Land of Sun & Gun. And it did.

With the saturation of lawyers there came a fierce competition to tango with justice, Florida-style. Lawyers, not available in stores, began to advertise on radio, on television, on bus benches, and on billboards. One attorney tried to entice new clients by offering to clean your windshield for free with every paid consultation. Need a lawyer while in Florida? Turn around, they're everywhere—pacing outside emergency rooms, graduating hourly from the Barbizon School of Law and Fashion, distributing business cards on the courthouse steps, chasing sunburned tourists across parking lots. The day of the locust has arrived.

The day I am waiting for is the day a lawyer botches a case for a client and the lust for the dollar overpowers professional cover-up. The day that lawyers begin suing each other. The day that a lawyer sues another for malpractice. I know—it sounds too much like science fiction.

Suffice it to say, even though some of my best friends know lawyers, I was not enthusiastic about the prospect of interviewing Wade Loftus, Entertainment and Sports Law. Despite the fact that I approached the assignment with an open mind and without any preconceived opinions.

• • •

The sun was glaring at streetlight level, making it impossible to discern the stop or go color. A taxi shot past me like a torpedo and almost broadsided an empty school bus that had just unloaded a pack of screaming moppets at the school yard. The smell of coffee was still fresh on my pants where I had spilled it pulling out of a McDonald's drive-thru. Salesmen were beginning their rounds. Housewives were slipping celebrity du jour workout tapes into VCRs. Seagulls laughed overhead. Palm fronds frolicked tauntingly in the breeze. Morning in the tropics.

I parked under a jacaranda tree in the parking lot of the law offices where Wade Loftus hung his shingle. Loftus shared a suite with two other independent attorneys.

It reminded me of the old Bob Newhart show where Bob the psychologist shared Carol the receptionist with Jerry the orthodontist and a urologist whose name I don't remember.

The receptionist was answering the phone as I walked in.

"Law offices," she said. The lawyers shared the same phone number. Generic law. "Hold, please." She pushed a couple buttons. "Line one, Ira. Your wife." She hung up and murmured, "Again." Noticing me for the first time, she flicked on her smile. "Can I help you?"

"I'd like to see Wade Loftus," I said.

"Really?" Her voice registered sincere disbelief, as if it wasn't the kind of request one would normally expect from a sane person. The receptionist's smile dissolved slowly before my eyes like the sun sinking into the gulf. Her eyes narrowed. She was reappraising me. Perhaps the magnificent vision standing in front of her wasn't the man of her dreams after all. Perhaps she had misjudged me. Perhaps I was a casually attired psycho juggler-acrobat who had spent five years perfecting his skills and the last twenty looking for a place to perform. And had finally snapped and was going to take it out on Wade Loftus, Entertainment Law. Perhaps that was what was going through the receptionist's mind. And for good reason. Chances of getting shot in a Florida law office by an unappreciative client were almost as great as getting blown away in a Kentucky post office by a deranged mail handler.

She kept staring at me, as if she wanted to say something but didn't quite know how.

If she was thinking what I thought she was thinking, I felt it my duty to put her at ease. "I'm unarmed," I said.

Her head tilted. She gave me a sidelong glance. "Excuse me?"

"I'm not a freelance wacko."

A puzzled gaze. "What are you talking about?"

Perhaps she wasn't thinking what I thought she was thinking. I read mail better than I read people.

"Never mind," I said. "I have a fertile imagination. I have trouble keeping a lid on it sometimes."

She smiled again. "Like now?"

"Good example. So do I get to see Loftus?"

"You don't have an appointment," she said matter-of-factly, without even glancing at her calendar.

"Is he busy?"

"Probably not."

"But I need an appointment?"

She shook her head. "No. That's not what I meant."

I had a sneaking suspicion she was subtly trying to steer me away from Wade Loftus—for my benefit.

I said, "I'm not a prospective client."

Her expression changed instantly from concern for the unsuspecting to relief. "May I tell him who's calling?"

"Harry Rice."

She picked up the phone and walked her fingers across some buttons. "Wade, there's a Harry Rice to see you." She bounced a pencil on its eraser while she waited for a response. "No. He's here now. Yes, Wade, standing next to me. I don't know. I'll ask him." She looked up at me. "Wade wants to know if you're listening." I nodded. "He's listening, Wade. What do you want me to do, tell him you're not in? No, Wade. Lying is not in my job description." She hung up and looked at me. "You sure you want to see him?"

"It's not a question of want."

She shrugged. "His office is the second door on the right."

"Are you in trouble with Wade now?"

"Like how?"

"Like blowing his cover."

"What's he going to do, fire me?"

"Well?"

"He's not going to fire me. The other two lawyers like me. Besides, Wade would be afraid to fire me. He thinks I know too much."

"Too much what?"

"Damned if I know."

Loftus's office was decorated in suitable-for-enshrinement basketball memorabilia. The walls were freckled with framed newspaper clippings extolling the accomplishments of sophomore all-conference forward Wade Loftus, a business major who was fourth in conference scoring. The few diplomas laminated on mahogany plaques were dwarfed by the centerpiece—a huge, framed jersey autographed by Meadowlark Lemon. Marble and bronze trophies cluttered the tops of bookcases filled with sports bios and several token legal volumes. Perched atop a filing cabinet was a glass-encased ABA basketball signed by Rick Barry. The den was more a monument to hoops than a legal practitioner's workshop. All that was missing were Magic Johnson's locker and Larry Bird's jockstrap.

At least Wade Loftus wasn't suited up in a Miami Heat uniform. He had on legal-guy togs—starched white shirt, red suspenders, paisley tie, emerald tie tack with matching cuff links. He did not stand or extend a hand. He stared at me, stone-faced.

"I know why you're here," he said dramatically. I think lawyers are onstage more than actors.

"I won't take much of your time."

"Sit down."

I sat. "I just need to ask you one question."

"You can ask, but I don't have to answer."

"No, you surely don't. You have the right to remain silent."

He strained to keep his composure. "Ask your question, Rice. I'm really not interested in jousting with you."

I settled back in the chair. "The night you came home and found the apartment empty, was the dead bolt locked?"

"Of course," he snorted.

"Now, see? That was painless, wasn't it? Thanks for your time, counselor."

There was a suspicious stirring behind his eyes. "That's it?"

"That's it."

"What good does that do you?"

I stood up. "Somebody had to have a key to relock the dead bolt. So that narrows down my investigation to whoever may have had access to your apartment keys."

His lip twitched slightly. Not much of a reaction, but enough.

"Wait a minute," he said, stalling as he sorted through the spasm of confusion. "I assume it was locked. I don't know for sure. I didn't check first. I just automatically put the key in and turned it. Maybe it wasn't locked."

"Did you feel or hear the dead bolt retract?"

"I don't remember." His expression was blank, but in his voice was irritation. "You know you shaved last Monday morning, but do you actually remember doing it? Let me ask you a question."

"Go."

"Do you remember my visit to your bar yesterday?"

"It changed my life." Little did I know at the time how prophetic that statement would be.

He glared icily at me. "You're really an amusing fellow, Rice. I want you to understand something from the beginning. This is the end. You are to stay out of my business.

You are to forget about my apartment. The break-in was reported to the police."

"I'm not so sure somebody broke in."

"You're not listening to me," he said sharply. "The insurance company honored its obligation. There is nothing further to be done."

"Your wife doesn't agree."

"It's not for her to agree or disagree. The point is, I will not have her throwing away my money on you. Not only is it baffling why she would want to, but it's downright irresponsible."

"You've got nothing to lose. If I don't recover the gun collection she doesn't owe me a cent."

He sat back smugly in his chair. "The gun collection? That's what this is about? Well, that's fine. That was my collection. Not hers. I had those guns before I had my first wife. Those guns are none of Eloise's business. And if they are none of her business, you can damn well be sure they are none of your business. Now get out of here. I have work to do."

"I don't recall seeing any clients lined up outside your door."

His nostrils flared, but his voice was controlled, almost patronizing. "I have a class to prepare for tonight."

I turned to leave. "I'll be in touch."

"Hey!"

I stopped and looked back at him.

"Let me give you some free legal advice."

"Are you qualified?"

"You don't want to test me, Rice. I'm not impressed with your comic-book, hard-boiled wisecracking P.I. routine. You stay out of my affairs or I'll have your ass in court."

I moved toward him, applying a full-court press, and eyed him steadily as I said, "Loftus, I didn't come here to find out if the dead bolt was locked. I came to see if it really would make you nervous to have someone poking around. I think it will."

Wade Loftus should have called for a time-out. Instead, he dribbled. "Butt out, Rice. I have friends who owe me favors. People you don't want to meet."

That one made me laugh. "Thanks, Wade. You just confirmed a theory. People with nothing to hide don't make threats."

"You've been warned," he said quietly, shaking his head.

"Yes I have, Wade. And I've been threatened before. I'm not afraid of your little friends. I'm not even afraid of going to court. In fact, I'll just bet that when I find out whatever it is you don't want me to find out, it will be you who doesn't want to go to court. Say hello to your wife for me."

five

·····

I left the law offices of Fender-bender and Associates, feeling as if I had just filed for ethical bankruptcy. I was in dire need of a moral transfusion. I knew just the place. Whenever my idea of humanity begins to decompose or I need to get my dignity out of hock, I go to the beach. It seldom fails to nourish any mental deficiency.

To the east a thin, incandescent curtain of clouds seemed to be melting into the horizon. Reflections of the high sun spangled off the turquoise sea. Beauty parlor darlings displayed colorfully decorated body parts like Christmas tree ornaments. People were laughing. Children were sifting sand through their fingers. In bars, genies were conjuring miracles in brown, long-necked bottles. In the shade, an aging beachboy wove palm baskets while his girlfriend swayed in a hammock strung between coconut palms. The silhouette of a seagull floated against the deep blue backdrop of the sky. Green needles of tall Australian pines aimed heavenward and shimmied in the breeze like mambo dancers. The sweet smell of salt air tugged at the tattered threads of responsibility, as my sense of duty washed out with the tide.

I can still find a monastic solitude on the shore to re-calibrate my shaken spirit. It doesn't matter what's going on around me. I can tune it out. With a childlike amazement I can watch in wonder as the sky changes colors throughout the day in a multitude of blue and pink and white and purple and red and orange tints that are found not in any art galleries, but only in the spectrum of God's radiant canvas. Then lights out and I take night walks along the water's edge, talking to ghosts I know can't hear me.

• • •

"We tried turning to Japanese cameras to save our marriage, even though I was the only one who knew it needed saving," said one of Father Shifty's parishioners.

She was a slender redhead wearing a minimalist bikini fashioned by Satan Dior.

Shifty could listen to the sob stories of his flock all day, as long as the customary donation was made—a shot of hooch and a chaser.

As Father Shifty once said to me, "Where else can a self-proclaimed sinner have their very own priest on retainer for less than ten percent?"

"Ex-priest," I reminded him.

He waved me off with a flick of his hand. "Still beats being a fundamentalist preacher. Besides, what's worse? Them going to church and telling lies to God, or coming here and swapping lies with me?"

"You know what would be better? You and Tammy Faye, together, serving up Sunday fried chicken and re-fried religion."

"Oh, Harry," sighed Father Shifty. "You mock me, son. Keep it up and I'll dislocate your tongue."

I believe he would have done it, too.

Carla was wiping the bar with a towel. Carla doesn't use rags.

"We blew a whole paycheck on the camera," said the redhead. "It was a beautiful machine."

Father Shifty nodded knowingly and dispensed a tolerant smile. That's his job. He was going to be busy with the redhead for a while.

I walked behind the bar and opened the cash register. There was enough change in it to get Carla through the afternoon. I asked her if she needed anything else.

"A raise," she said. "Six weeks' paid vacation. A retirement system. A dental plan. An employee cafeteria. More breaks."

We compromised on another day of job security.

I poured myself a shot from a bottle of Maker's Mark. The moral transfusion.

After that I drove to the campus to see my client, Eloise Loftus.

• • •

Was a time when college students dressed in Army-Navy surplus, granny dresses, cords, bell-bottom jeans, beads, silver boots, and leather sandals. The talk was of revolution, reform, Angela Davis, sharing the land, loving, and acceptance. Phi Beta Kappa was rejected as elitist. Texts, published solely to prevent perish, were tossed. Young scholars carried manifesto projectors from one mind-expanding experience to another.

The students I saw and heard as I walked across the campus were decked out in designer jumpsuits and hundred-dollar running shoes. Boy marketing majors were sweet-talking girl shopping majors. The biggest concern facing the nation was the rising price of designer jeans. Not crime, not the ecology or the environment. Underarm they carried the latest best-selling pop psychology and self-help books.

I asked a coed coming out of the school bookstore for directions to the Humanities Department. A delicate smile blossomed before my eyes.

She pointed to a building across the quadrangle. "It's the double doors under the portico," she said.

I was thinking of ways to show her my appreciation without getting arrested when a young beefcake dressed in Hush Puppies, pleated jeans, and a European pullover came out of the bookstore. He took my guide by the arm. As he led her away he sneered at me the way his father might sneer at a man without credit.

A bell rang, disgorging somnolent students from cubbyholes. I made my way through the crowding corridor toward the Humanities Department.

Two campus cops were coming out of the doors with frosted, pebbled-glass windows. DEPARTMENT OF HUMANITIES was stenciled in black across the pane. The reception area was receptionistless. A black-and-white wall directory listed the teachers' names and office numbers.

I found the office I was looking for at the end of a hall. It was a small room, maybe ten by twelve, and could barely contain the scent of the jasmine sprigs sticking out of a glass cup that sat on top of a file cabinet. A pinch of femininity amidst the ruins. Everything else was strictly academics. The room was cluttered with books stuffed in crannies, overflowing from bookcases, stacked on top of every horizontal surface. Books were piled on the floor and boxed in cardboard. Scattered papers and fanned student files were strewn about the desk.

Eloise Loftus sat behind her desk as motionless as a store mannequin. She stared musingly at her lap. She had on a simple white dress with green piping, and looked vulnerable, like a damsel in wait for a knight errant.

"Need a dragon slain?" I said.

Her head twitched as if she had been caught in mid-thought. She laid her dark eyes on me. She said neither yes nor no, but her lips parted just enough to make me feel heroic.

"They say things come in threes, Mr. Rice," she said after a disarmingly long silence. She rolled her head back, stretched her neck. With her eyes closed she asked, "What's it like outside?"

"A Chamber of Commerce day."

She opened her eyes and did a slow turn in my direction. "Good. Care for a walk?"

"Sure."

She led me across the grass, past the library. Sun-blanched student bodies sprawled on the lawn, leaned against trees, or wandered aimlessly, like dust mites. A few lolled against the library as if they could absorb the contents of the building by osmosis.

We strolled along a promenade that framed a rectangular pond.

Eloise Loftus said, "The students say there's a caiman living in the pond."

"Has anyone seen it, or is this the school's version of the Loch Ness monster legend?"

"There are some who claim to have seen the snout break water. No one has ever seen the whole thing." She stopped walking. "You're the detective; tell me—how do you prove, or disprove, the presence of an unseen danger?"

"Well," the detective ventured, "I'd send out a trial balloon."

She smiled. "That's why I believe there's a caiman in the water."

"I'll bite."

"Your trial balloons. Look around. What's missing?"

She let me think about that as we started walking again. I drew a blank. "Ducks," she said. "Where did the ducks go? There used to be ducks here." We exchanged glances. "Why are you here, Mr. Rice?"

"Is the formality necessary?"

She considered that for longer than I thought was necessary. Perhaps for her the boundary between informality and formality wasn't as hazy as it was for me.

"You don't work with contracts, do you?" she said.

"No."

"Ever have trouble collecting?"

"No."

"Really?" She sounded surprised.

"No. I just don't think contracts would make a difference. If someone isn't inclined to pay you, their signature on a dotted line isn't going to make a difference. And I don't sue people. So I just rely on instinct. The couple times I got stiffed, I expected it."

"Then why did you take those jobs?"

"Something my uncle told me once. After I got out of the service I was struggling along on the GI Bill, trying to get through college. My uncle helped out by writing the checks for the tuition. I promised him I would pay him back some day. He said he didn't want my money. He said, Just remember that as you go through life there have been, and always will be, people who have helped you. That'll be true all your life, Harry, he said. It's true of all of us. Age doesn't change that. There are times when we all need help. He said, Remember as you go along and come across someone in need, hold out your hand. You do that, he said, and I'll have been repaid."

"Paid in full?"

"I'm still working on the interest. I doubt if I'll ever be able to pay off the principal. There have been too many people that have helped me over the years."

"I like that answer. Harry."

"Thank you. Eloise."

We looked at each other.

"Now we're informal," she said. "What's next? Do you send me flowers?"

I didn't have a bon mot ready for that one. Whenever I'm stumped for repartee, which is more often than I care to admit, I rely on an old trick that never fails. I change the subject.

"What about threes?" I said.

"Hmmm?"

"In your office, you said something about things coming in threes."

"I did, didn't I. Did you happen to pass the campus police when you came in?"

"Yes."

"They were coming from my office. It was burglarized last night. I can already hear the wheels of your detective mind at work. But it doesn't appear to have been students looking for test answers or anything like that. None of my class papers were disturbed. Some of my personal belongings and mementos were taken. Pictures, knick-knacks, things of value only to me."

"That's two. Your apartment and now your office. You expect something else?"

"It's three. Several weeks ago, on our wedding anniversary to be exact, my car was stolen while I was at the spa."

"You think there's a relation among the three events?"

"No, of course not. I just meant, bad luck seems to come grouped in threes." Then she changed the subject. "Wade called me."

"He told you I visited his office this morning?"

"Yes. Was that necessary?"

"I think so." I let it go at that for the time being. I had

my doubts about him, but nothing I could sing with a tune.

"All right. What else? Are you here to give me a progress report?"

I laughed. "Actually, more of a no-progress report. I had some questions I wanted to ask you."

"Ask away."

"According to the police report, you were in Gainesville the week the apartment was burglarized."

"I was."

"Who knew you were out of town?"

"Why? Do you think it was someone we know?"

"Eloise, at this point I don't know enough to think anything."

"Of course. You're just being thorough. It's that there was no sign of breaking in, isn't it? That bothers me, too. Let me think. Wade, of course, knew I was gone. I was on summer break, so no one at school would have known. Mrs. Robinette, the widow across the hall, knew I was gone. I may have told Ted Kanecki, but I don't remember doing so. He's the building manager. I usually call and let him know if I'm going to be away. I think that's all. It was really on short notice. My cousin had an appendectomy."

"Would Wade have told anyone else?"

"You'd have to ask him, but I'd rather you left him out of this if you can. He seems bothered by it all." She checked her watch. "I'm sorry, Harry, but I've got an appointment in a couple minutes with a student. Walk me back to my office."

As we walked back to the office, I asked her to call Ted Kanecki, the building manager, for me. "Let him know I'll be coming by to ask some questions. I want you to give him authorization to let me into your apartment. I want to see the locks. If he reacts to your request in any way unusual, too willing or too reluctant to accommodate, let me know. Also let him know I'll be canvassing some of your neighbors."

"All right. Anything else?"

"Probably. But that's all for now."

We stopped in front of the Humanities office.

"Call me," she said.

"I will."

Before I left the campus, I decided to stop and see if my friend Mali was in her office. I cut across the lawn toward the English Department. It had been a few weeks since I had talked to Mali. Too long. I couldn't remember our having gone so long without speaking. Even if it was just a phone call to check in and see how the other was doing. But time can get away. The fact that I hadn't kept in touch with her didn't mean that I had forgotten about her. Truth was, I couldn't not think about her; I couldn't get her out of my mind. There were momentary diversions, like work, but she had a hold on me I couldn't break. There are some memories that I just couldn't banish to the unconscious zone.

The reason I mention this is that I did see Mali that day. We didn't speak, though. In fact, she didn't see me. I ran out of things to say before we even started, when I saw her walking hand in hand around the pond with another man.

Why did it bother me? Had I been hoping she'd eventually get Chuckie out of her system and we'd be able to recapture what we once had?

It puzzled me, but not nearly as much as it hurt.

six

. . . .

As I drove away from the campus I was nailed with the same numbness I had experienced years earlier.

Her name was Theresa. I met her about a year after my divorce. We fell in love. One of those corny made-for-each-other love affairs that would never end. The kind of love that teenagers feel every four or five weeks, the "real thing." I didn't know it could be so good or so right. Nothing could separate us. Until Theresa went for her annual physical.

Two days later her doctor called with the test results. I can still hear the ring from that phone call. He told her to check into the hospital immediately. She would never check out. She was dead in less than a month. Cancer.

Looking back, I can't recall having left that hospital room at all during that time, but I know I did. Theresa and I talked about a lot of things. Except maybe the things we should have been talking about. Did I ever really tell her how important she was to me? How much I loved her? Did I even know the words to express those feelings? Maybe she knew, but that's not good enough. I left too many things unsaid. I still do that. Instead, I sat there while she comforted me. She was dying, and she was worried about me. I assured her that I was strong and would be fine. She knew me better than I knew myself.

I prayed. I offered God a trade. Me for Theresa. No deal. When she died I was numb. Dead souls feel no pain.

Don't make promises that can't be kept. Theresa made me promise not to close myself off from the rest of the world.

"No walls," she said.

"No walls," I agreed.

What I thought was mourning turned out to be withdrawal. I had convinced myself that I was doing fine. I was a functioning member of society. I was working. I said hello. And I ran away if someone said, How you doing? That was too intimate. That's the way it was until I met Mali. We became friends. I don't know why Mali. It's one of those inexplicable phenomenons that occur rarely in a lifetime. You meet a person and you just know that there's a kindred spirit. A trust developed, an instant intimacy, and I heard myself telling Mali things that I hadn't told anyone, not even myself. About lugging around a heart filled with tears, a heart that kept getting heavier. Where was the release valve?

It wasn't until Mali started helping me remove the bricks that I realized I had built a wall. I told myself Theresa would understand the need for a temporary barrier. As the wall came down I discovered I was able to fall in love again. It was good while it lasted. Just the three of us. Me and Mali and Chuckie's shadow. When it was over, I could deal with it because I still had Mali my friend. I hadn't lost that. But now, after seeing her with another man, I had a panic attack. I thought, Jesus, I'm not going to lose Mali, too?

The numbness.

I have a tendency to overreact. So I'm told. I convinced

myself not to blow anything out of proportion. Take your mind off it. Get back to work.

• • •

Sam Maturano's Old Stuff was located in the antique district of Dania, a small town on the Florida gold coast, where men still went to barbershops for haircuts and a GED recipient could be elected mayor. Unlike many small towns, there were no abandoned churches, movie theaters, cottages, or storefronts along Dania's chunk of U.S. 1. Except for the Greek restaurant and the orange-painted pharmacy that sold more plastic lawn flamingos than aspirins, the string of commercial and once-residential buildings and houses of worship were all crammed with expensive hand-me-downs and orphaned crap.

Dania was a misplaced southern town purged of Bible Belt sentiment. "Rock of Ages" had been replaced by "Money" as the town's anthem, and everyone sang its praises. There were almost as many old DeSotos and Packards parked diagonally on the side streets as there were new Mercurys and Buicks. I parked my car on the shale alley behind Sam's.

A brass bell, nailed to the door, rang as I went in. The outer room was an inventory of smells—old leather, waxed woods, greasy hatbands, aged newsprint—that, when combined, effected a single musty odor. I looked around at the old pictures, the lace high-neck blouses, the chinaware, the yellowed linen, the jewelry, the cameos, and the hand-crafted furniture. Old Stuff was a metaphoric spoor of previous generations, a morgue of dead reveries.

Sam was standing behind the counter, holding an art deco lamp. He was talking to an old woman with hunched shoulders.

"That's the best price you'll ever get," he was saying. "Go ahead and look elsewhere if you don't believe me."

Judging from the look on the woman's face, she didn't believe him.

"But if you do," Sam warned, "it's at your peril. I can't guarantee the lamp will be here when you come back. And you will come back. You know why?"

The woman shook her head.

"I'm selling it at cost," Sam explained. "I don't do this to make money. I already have enough money for two lifetimes. I just like working with antiques. I like seeing people get what they want without being robbed. That's what makes me happy. That's why I do this."

I felt like introducing Sam to Father Shifty. They could take turns canonizing each other.

The skeptical shopper took the lamp from Sam and looked it over. "I don't know," she said. "It looks like a reproduction to me."

Without missing a beat Sam said, "Of course it's a reproduction. You think I could sell it that cheap if it was authentic?"

The old woman placed the lamp on the counter. "I think I better look around some more."

"Sure," Sam said, exasperated. "Look around. Spend more money than you should and then cry poor to Congress so they can raise my taxes to give you more social security. What the hey. I'm just the middleman. I'll tell you what. It's cheaper for me to take the loss now than to have to pay higher taxes. I'll knock ten dollars off the price. I might as well eat it now than feed it to the tax man later."

The woman plucked some bills from her beaded purse before Sam could change his mind. Lamp in hand, she waddled out the door with a sly grin. If Sam was in business to make people happy, he was succeeding.

Turning to me, Sam said, "You Harry Rice, or do you just look like him?"

"It ain't been that long, Sam."

"You sound like my wife," he deadpanned. "I have to go a year before I know I'm cut off."

He came out from behind the counter with his hand held out. It had probably been three years since I had last seen Sam. He looked the same. He was wearing a rumpled sweatshirt, as usual, and his khaki pants hung so low you wondered what kept them up. He had no ass, but an ample gut. His head was covered with a welter of red hair that kept falling over his blue eyes like the mane of a shaggy dog. With his fingers he combed a shock of hair back over his forehead.

"Last I heard, you had sold your detective agency and bought a bar," Sam said. "Come on in the back."

I followed him through a bamboo curtain into the back room.

"Yeah, I did," I said. "But I'm back doing investigations."

"The bar go under?"

"No. Just doing both."

"Sit down." He sank into a tufted leather armchair. I sat on a hard ladder-back. "You marry again?"

"No," I said. "I still haven't found the foot that fits the glass slipper."

"You looking?"

"I'm not sure."

"Anyone special?"

"I'm not sure." I was getting uncomfortable with this line of questioning. I was the one who was supposed to be asking questions. "So how are things with you, Sam?"

"Me? Great. What could go wrong? My life has no moving parts."

I laughed. "What about the wife?"

"She thinks she's a tollbooth."

"No free rides?"

"You got it. I got a daughter who wants to quit college and be a *Solid Gold* dancer. I got a boy who can't get auto insurance. The only pal I had, my dog, Sam Jr., died. Let me tell you, that was incredibly painful."

"I know the feeling. Pooh-Pooh died a few weeks ago."

"That cat you had?"

I nodded.

"Damn. I'd a thought she died years ago. How old was she?"

"Sixteen. She'd been with my daughter since the divorce. You know any stray cats looking for a home?"

"No. I don't stock them. That's not my line."

"What is your line, Sam? You still the gun expert?"

"Aha! That's what this is all about. Silly me. I thought you were being sociable. You're working a case."

Without mentioning names I told Sam about the missing gun collection. I showed him a copy of the list Eloise Loftus had given me.

"My client says a hundred thousand."

Sam gave me a noncommittal glance. He slipped on a pair of thick, black-framed glasses that might have once belonged to Buddy Holly or Woody Allen. He perused the list, bouncing his head to some private beat. Finally he took off his glasses and laid them on his lap.

"You understand, Harry, with any collectible the numero uno factor is always condition. The condition of any item can easily increase or decrease its valuation by fifty percent or more."

"Are you saying all the guns would have to be in mint condition for that inventory to be worth a hundred grand?"

"Frankly, I don't see a hundred thousand dollars here,

even if we assumed all the guns were in excellent condition. That's on a quick reading, now. I could be wrong. Remember, I haven't dealt guns for quite a few years. Still, most of these guns would be categorized modern. A lot of vintage war weapons from Europe. Those guns have been decreasing in value the last eight or nine years."

"Decreasing? I thought the value increased with age."

"Normally that's true of most things, but not hookers and guns."

"Explain."

"Sometime around 'eighty-four or 'eighty-five, the U.S. eased its restrictions for importing guns. Naturally there was an influx of guns that used to be hard to get. Especially military guns, which have been pouring in ever since. Supply and demand. As the supply exceeded the demand, prices fell. These prices on your list may have been accurate ten years ago, but not today."

"Is the collection worthless?"

"No, it's not worthless. There are a couple of antiques and a few curios, but mostly it's just a collection of moderns and commemoratives. The market on commemorative issues isn't that good anymore, either. Most commemoratives still sell for more than the original issue price, but they no longer command some of the prices that they used to. And in some cases that's even true of curios."

"What's a curio? And an antique, for that matter."

"An antique is easy. Something before 1900. Actually, it's more like 1898. The curio is kind of a hard classification. It's a legal classification used by Alcohol, Tobacco and Firearms. A curio has to be fifty years old and uncommon, rare. Basically, it's a category used for collectors so they can ship weapons interstate. Collectors have to be licensed by ATF to do that."

I scanned the list. "Any curios on this?"

Sam put on his glasses and bounced his eyes up and down the list. "Offhand, the Yato thirty-two. It's a Japanese semiautomatic handgun. This century. Probably categorized as a military curio. Same for several of the Lugers."

"What about that other category?"

"Commemoratives? Yeah. The Magna-Port Five is one. I used to have one. It's a western-style single action revolver. It's American. A Ruger, forty-four caliber. But ever since Bicentennial fever, when everybody and their grandmother started issuing commemoratives, the bottom has fallen out of that market, too."

I thought about what Sam had said for a moment. Then I asked, "Is there anything of real value here?"

"Again, Harry, this is all off the top of my head."

"I understand."

"All right. I would say that the M-seventy-eight Mauser Zig Zag could bring six, seven thousand dollars if it's in excellent condition. The turret pistol is definitely an antique and could bring as much as ten thousand dollars, depending on condition. Why don't you give me some time to check out your list with several price guides and dealers I know? I'll put out some feelers for you and maybe in between selling antique VCRs I might find a lead for you."

"That'd be nice. Want a copy of the list?"

Sam got up and walked over to a support pole in the center of the room. He took a clipboard off a hook and flipped through several pages.

"This past June, the Loftus collection?" Whatever look I gave him made him laugh. "Every dealer and former dealer in the area got a copy. The police think we have nothing better to do than look out for stolen merchandise."

Our business over and a customer waiting, Sam walked me to the door.

"I'll appreciate anything you can find out for me, Sam."

"You will? Enough to give me a finder's fee if I get anything?"

"I wouldn't insult you like that, Sam. You've got enough money to last you two lifetimes. I'm letting you do this because it makes you happy."

seven

········

That would have been the time to quit. If Sam was right, and the guns were overvalued, my take of the recovered value could be nominal and not worth the time and effort expended. Yeah, I should have stopped then. That's what common sense dictated. But when a situation calls for common sense, I sometimes have a tendency to employ moronic logic. I convinced myself that I was not a mercenary. I didn't work just for money. There were more than monetary rewards to be considered. So what was I considering? Well, let's put it this way—would I have stayed on the case if Eloise Loftus looked like Larry Csonka?

I doubt it.

• • •

Less than an hour after leaving Sam's Old Stuff I was in Hallandale on my way to inspect the Loftus condominium.

Chez Loftus was two blocks north of the Hallandale Beach Boulevard drawbridge, situated between A1A and the intracoastal waterway. I parked in a visitor's slot and followed a Chattahoochee walk to an alcove lined with mailboxes and a bulletin board plastered with pertinent reminders of a long-past owners' meeting and the importance of cleaning lint traps after each load of laundry.

The manager's office was on the ground level near the elevator shaft. I rang the bell.

"It's open. Let yourself in," called a distant voice.

It was a no-frills office with a gray government surplus desk and matching swivel chair. Against a wall was a library table with stacks of paperback books and a sign that read: TAKE ONE—LEAVE ONE. No plants. No make-yourself-at-home-and-stay-awhile chairs. Do your business and leave. Even the paneled walls were bare, save for a lone bank calendar to break up the empty space. It reminded me of a conversation I had with a neighbor's kid a few years ago. I had been in my backyard, pruning a ficus tree, wearing cutoffs and no shirt. The kid came over to visit. He liked to talk baseball with me since we were both Oriole fans. Somewhere in the middle of fielding strategies and base running blunders there was a lull in the conversation. To fill the gap the kid suddenly says, "I wonder why God put tits on men." He seemed to understand that women needed them for nursing babies and consoling grown men, but why did men have them? What purpose did they serve? I didn't have an answer, but he did. He said, "You know, I'll bet it's for the same reason you hang pictures on a wall."

Behind the desk was a hallway, which I supposed led to the manager's living quarters. I could hear the sounds of something sizzling in a frying pan and someone rummaging through a utensil drawer.

"What can I do for you?" called the voice from the back.

"I'm Harry Rice."

"You the one Mrs. Loftus called about?"

"Yes."

"Where did you park?"

"Visitor slot."

"You didn't back in, did you?"

"No."

Ted Kanecki sauntered in, wiping his hands on a dish towel. He was slope-shouldered and wiry and gave the impression of being taller than he was. He wore a white polo shirt with the condo's logo, and hemmed beige shorts. His face was expressionless, his voice a monotone.

"Here's the key," he said. "Apartment four-oh-nine. Lock it when you're done and return the key." He turned to leave, then stopped. "You need me for anything?"

I asked him a few questions. He told me that the spare apartment keys were kept in a sturdy combination safe. No one else knew the combination. In the event of Ted Kanecki's demise the combination was in a safe-deposit box at a local bank and would be released to the condo's board of directors. Ted Kanecki told me with his only show of emotion that the week of the burglary he had been in Alabama burying an old army buddy who had committed suicide.

"The Army killed him. They wouldn't leave him alone. It started in Vietnam. He got in a lot of trouble because he was hanging around Buddhist monks and trading dirty words like peace and freedom. They gave him a general discharge, man. Less than honorable. Man couldn't work. The Army beat him. Vietcong couldn't do it, so the fucking Army killed him."

I had heard similar stories and believed every one of them.

• • •

The floor was antique-white ceramic tile. A harvest of modern furniture sprouted from it like the malignant-looking sculptures typically found outside federal buildings, and looked just about as comfortable. One wall was an electronic jungle of audio and video components. Apartment 409 reeked of floral soap balls.

I checked out all the doors and windows. A sliding glass door led to a fourth-story balcony overlooking A1A. The door was well secured with a dowel rod and a steel pin. The front door dead bolt was heavy duty and could only be locked and unlocked with a key, both in- and outside. Overall, the security was better than average and would keep out amateurs and kids. The windows were plate glass except for a bank along the bottom, about eighteen inches high, that opened. Too narrow to squeeze a sofa through.

Theoretically, the furniture could have been hoisted over the balcony railing and lowered to the parking lot with a pulley, but it would have been too cumbersome and visible. No, the only way would have been to take everything out the front door, down the hall to the freight elevator at the end of the corridor. It could not be done inconspicuously. I looked around the living room one last time. No sinister shadows or eerie noises.

As I left the apartment, the door across the hall closed quickly. The telltale sign of a snooping neighbor. Just the kind of neighbor I wanted to talk to. I locked 409, stepped across the hall, and knocked.

A voice responded immediately, not more than a door's width away. "What do you want?"

I flashed my most angelic smile at the peephole. "I'd like to talk to you for a few minutes."

"You selling?" A gravel voice.

"No. I'm working for Mrs. Loftus. I'm a private investigator."

"What is your name?" A hint of a New England accent.

"Harry Rice."

"All right, Harry Rice. I'm going to call Eloise at school. If she doesn't know you I'm calling the police."

I stood awkwardly in the hall, feeling like a wolf in sheep's clothing, wondering if my angelic smile resembled a devilish grin. Finally the door opened.

She couldn't have been a day under eighty or an inch over five feet. She didn't try to disguise her age with makeup or dye, which is not to say she was unkempt. She wore a simple cotton dress. Her face was alert and intense. She raised her blue eyes to mine. "You look harmless enough," she said. "Come in."

"No police?"

"It's still up for consideration." I followed her into the living room. She pointed to an end table with a phone off its cradle. "Eloise wants to talk to you."

I sat on the edge of a wicker love seat and picked up the phone. "Hello."

"Hi, Harry. I see you've met Mrs. Robinette."

"Sort of."

"Don't underestimate her and don't talk to her like she's a dotty old woman. Her mind is razor sharp. She's a retired lecturer. Women's studies."

"Sounds like you're warning me."

"It seems like I am, doesn't it. She was a feminist before it was even a word. I know almost all of her spiels by heart: Men are predictable. They will try to control women any way they can. Whatever it takes. They'll try coddling. They'll try crying. They'll stoop to sarcasm and self-pity and mockery and guilt and sex and hate."

"I'm so ashamed."

Eloise laughed. "Hang your head when you say that, mister. Don't get me wrong, though. She's really a wonderful lady. Just don't say anything that can be interpreted as sexist."

"I'll pray to God that She gives me the wisdom to be politically correct."

"You learn fast. Listen, Harry, before I hang up there's something I wanted to mention to you. Maybe it's nothing more than coincidence, I don't know. Yesterday was Wade's birthday. We didn't celebrate it yesterday because he had to teach a class here last night."

The way she stopped, I assumed that was supposed to have been important. "Am I missing something?" I said.

"I'm not sure. Remember, my car was stolen on our anniversary, and now my office was broken into on Wade's birthday."

Ah! The old significant-dates theory. Nothing gets past the veteran detective. "Gotcha," I said. "What about June twenty-eighth?"

"Besides the robbery, nothing."

"You sure? No goldfish birthdays or anything?"

"Bastard. I hope Mrs. Robinette tears you to shreds." At least she was laughing when she said it. We hung up.

I sat back. Mrs. Robinette was sitting upright on a bentwood rocker. Her hands were resting on her lap. Portrait of the suffragette as an old woman. She had listened intently to my end of the phone conversation.

She frowned. "What did she say about me?"

"She told me not to talk to you as if you were a dotty old woman. She said you would try to manipulate me by using fear and sex and rotten cooking. She said I should watch out for you."

Her eyes sparkled with smug satisfaction. "Do you have the courage, Harry Rice, to face the abyss?"

"Face the abyss," I repeated. "Erik Estrada?"

She smiled for the first time. "Nietzsche."

"Ray Nietzsche? Green Bay Packers?"

"Hardly. What do you want to know?"

"I want to know about June twenty-eighth."

"The day the police came."

"Yes."

"Are you sure you want to know about that day?"

I know a loaded question when I hear one. "Is there some other day I should know about?"

"Ask me about two days before the police came."

"The twenty-sixth? What happened two days before the police came?"

"That was the day I saw the movers take everything out of the apartment."

"The twenty-sixth?"

"Yes."

"The police report said—"

"I know what I saw and when I saw it. It was the twenty-sixth. Now ask me about the twenty-fourth."

"You're good at my job. How about if I stop asking questions and you tell me what you know."

She took a deep breath, like a lecturer about to go on-stage. "I know that Mr. Loftus brought a young woman home with him the night after Eloise went to Gainesville. She was much younger than Mr. Loftus. She could have been his daughter. She was back with him again the next night. The twenty-fifth. The day after that the movers came. There were two men—boys, actually. Maybe twenty years old. They looked Latin. The girl wasn't with them. That night Mr. Loftus came home from work and went into the apartment. He came back out, looked up and down the hall. He went back inside. A few minutes later I heard him come out and lock his door. Two days later, the twenty-eighth, he came home from work at his usual time. About an hour later the police came."

"Why didn't you tell the police this?"

"They only wanted to know if I had seen anything that day, the twenty-eighth. I told them no. I started to tell them about the twenty-sixth, but they cut me off like I was a senile old biddy. They were too busy and too important to indulge me."

I nodded. "The know-it-all badge mentality. I know it well." I looked at her. "Did you talk to the movers?"

"No."

"Did you call the police when you saw the movers?"

"No reason to. They looked legitimate. They wore coveralls, some kind of uniform. They were not being secretive about it. They must have let themselves into the apartment with a key. I didn't hear anything that sounded like a break-in."

"How's your hearing?"

"Not as good as it was," she admitted. She wasn't offended by the question. "I did call the manager's office to check on the movers."

"But he was out of town."

"That's correct." For a moment she was meditative. And then she said, "I guess it was wishful thinking."

"How's that?"

"I thought maybe Eloise was leaving him."

I leaned forward and said, "What about the woman Mr. Loftus brought home. What can you tell me about her?"

"She was young. Platinum blond."

"Tall? Thin? Color of eyes?"

"I didn't get that close. The peephole in the door makes people look like images in a fun-house mirror."

"Anything else I should know?"

"It would be personal."

I smiled at her. "You haven't told anyone else this, have you?"

"I mind my own business," she said swiftly.

I couldn't help but laugh, which she took as rude.

"What's so funny?" She sounded indignant.

"Don't you see the contradiction? A busybody who minds her own business?"

"You asked if I told anyone." There was an edge to her voice. "I said no. You are confusing a busybody with a gossip."

I nodded. "I do that a lot. My apologies."

She accepted.

"Why did you tell me?" I said.

She shrugged. "Eloise hired you. That means she wants to know what happened. And I suppose I think it's time she did know."

• • •

When I left Mrs. Robinette, the better part of the day was gone. It had been a productive day. I had learned that Wade Loftus had been bouncing a Lolita off his face while his wife was away, which explained in part his opposition to Eloise's hiring me. I had learned that the date of the burglary was June 26 and not the twenty-eighth. Maybe the twenty-sixth was another meaningful date in the life and times of the Loftus clan. I learned that the guns were not as valuable as I would have liked. And I learned that Mali wasn't scrubbing floors in a convent, pining for the man that got away.

It had been a productive day. But not a happy one.

eight

•••••••

I spent the next day looking through haystacks for an elusive needle with a thread of connection to the missing Loftus household effects. I scoured dozens of pawnshops, consignment shops, and used furniture stores, trying to match anything to the descriptions on the inventory list Eloise Loftus had provided to her insurance company. After ten monotonous hours the net result of my work was zilch. Even lunch had been a washout. I had a fruit platter that tasted like, and was about as fresh as, a Cézanne painting. Those kinds of days are typical in the investigation business. When they happen I just return to the beach and lick my wounds.

At twilight, the narrow alley behind the Sand Bar resembles a long dark hall with walls of salt-air-eroded Vacancy signs and weather-bleached cottages and motels. Along this span are brightly painted Dumpsters and trash cans. Beach garbage is better dressed than the homeless who rummage through these private dining rooms for leftovers. An overpowering odor of fried seafood and dried urine hovered over the macadam alley that runs parallel with the Broadwalk.

I parked in my reserved slot behind the Sand Bar. As I got out of my car I noticed a candy-apple red Corvette across the alley. It was one of those classic models from the early sixties. The door of the 'Vette swung open. A long, naked leg slipped out seductively, like the limb of a striptease dancer slithering through the slit in a sequined gown. A second leg emerged. Twins. I was in no hurry. I stood by, wondering if the rest of the vision would be worth the wait.

It was. She could have been a dancer in Elvis's 1968 TV comeback special. She was dressed in black hot pants, a vest that was skimpier than most suspenders, and a black leather belt that Elvis would have envied. A lot of skin on display. Her face was partially obliterated by a wild mass of thick black hair. She saw me admiring her. She stared at me through the dim light of sunset. Her green eyes glowed like a cat's in heat. A twentieth-century witch as the temptress.

She approached me slowly, almost cautiously. With each step she came more into focus. I surveyed the swells of her hips with all the appreciation of an art major. Her breasts were slight, but worn like expensive pendants. She was Botticelli's Venus grown up in 3-D. My compliments to the sculptor. She was sensual and spiritual and I was a blithering idiot.

She stood in front of me. Her vampire-red lips parted. We were so close that I could feel the kiss of her warm breath on my cheek. This woman could be trouble. I could do one of two things: yield to lust or do the smart thing, which I wasn't at all familiar with.

She smiled. My pulse rate doubled.

"Harry," she said softly. "Is that you, honey?"

I was afraid if I spoke I would slobber on her.

"It is you," she said. There were sketches of Spain in the way she talked.

She made me glad it was me. She began to hug me. Her hips buffeted against my groin. My gratitude began to rise.

"It's been so long," she whispered in my ear.

All I could think was, who is this? Not that it mattered. Then we were kissing, her breasts pushing against mine. Our tongues danced as my fingers eased down the silky skin of her back, anticipating their next course. She clutched my buttocks in both hands. I did not play hard to get. It was strictly a case of prurient submission. I was living proof that if you lead a man by his gonads his heart and mind will follow.

She pulled away and combed a hand through her tangled hair.

First there was the glint of the shiny steel. Then the cold edge of the blade. It was as sudden and as skillful as a Las Vegas magician's sleight of hand. It was over just as quickly. She pushed the knife into my mouth and with a flick she pulled the blade out, slicing the inside of my upper lip. Not a wasted move. Professional.

I tasted copper and felt warm blood brimming at my lips before the stinging sensation kicked in with a jolt. My tongue penetrated an incision that felt the size of a bubbling hot tub of Bloody Marys. It's always more exaggerated when it's your blood.

Gripping the knife tightly, she pressed the point of the blade against the base of my neck. I could feel the sharpness all the way down my legs.

She looked at me for a long time. "Forget about the guns," she advised. She was as serious as a doctor prescribing a life-saving diet. She dragged the knife up, scratching my neck. *"Comprende?"*

"I get the point," I gurgled, swallowing a mouthful of blood.

Jacqueline the Ripper kissed her trigger finger and then touched my bloody lips with it.

"I hope so." She sounded sincere.

Still holding the knife out, she stepped away. She walked backward, into the shadows, until she was just an apparition.

• • •

In one corner of the emergency room a squad of sociopaths were comparing scars. A man with a hairweave, dressed in sweat, grease, and denim, was leaning against a wall, his face a grotesque contortion of agony. He was holding up a hand wrapped in a blood-soaked towel. A fat woman sat in front of a television, staring at a sitcom, oblivious to the wails of the baby she was holding. Next to a magazine table, a frail woman held an ice pack to her swollen nose. Beside her was a grim, large man with a look that dared anyone to tell him she didn't have it coming.

A screeching siren announced the arrival of another ambulance with a fresh load. Brisk orderlies wheeled in a gurney on which an old woman writhed. A serious and efficient nurse quickly took the patient to a private area. Nurses and orderlies were the only medical players among the pandemonium. I imagined the doctors were holed up in a back room throwing darts at a diagnosis chart. Hospitals would probably run better if they were turned over to the nurses. You'll never hear me speak ill of the nursing profession. I have the same admiration and weakness for nurses that I have for barmaids. Nurses and barmaids both administer to my pain. They are my demon-killers.

I had been waiting my turn for about ten minutes when I started choking and coughing. I looked for a receptacle. Not even an ashtray. I discharged a coagulated glob of blood the size of a plum tomato onto the floor. A solemn-faced nurse ran over, grabbed my arm, and led me to an empty area behind a curtain. She sat me on an aluminum table and placed a spit pan on my lap.

"Don't worry," she said, patting my hand reassuringly. "A doctor will be with you in a moment."

"Busy night?" I mumbled.

"No. Actually this is quiet for us."

She left. The spit pan came in handy. I sat for over an hour, waiting. Finally a scrawny man with a Fu Manchu mustache pulled open the curtain. He was wearing a black T-shirt and faded jeans. He had doper's eyes and looked like an escapee from the sociopath group.

He looked at me and didn't seem pleased with what he saw. He glanced at a slip of paper he was holding. He looked at me again. "You're not a black female, are you?"

I shook my head, my identity crisis resolved.

He appeared to be mesmerized by the caked blood around my mouth. Without asking, he turned up my lip like a vet checking a horse's teeth.

"It looks worse than it is." He looked over my lip. "You been chewing on bottles?"

It's hard to answer when your lip is being held up over your nose.

"A cleaning, a little dressing, maybe a couple stitches or more. You'll be all right. Just have to smile with one lip for a while. I'm sure there must be a Zen instructional book on that." He was saying all of this as he pulled some surgical stuff and needles and vials from a drawer.

This was the doctor. I have known loan sharks who have inflicted less pain.

nine

• • • • • •

The absurd image in the mirror looked like Mortimer Snerd. My upper lip jutted out to the extent that I could have rented it as a beach umbrella.

It was still dark when I got out of bed. It had been a sleepless night. I had swallowed enough blood and pride that my gut felt like the inside of a public toilet. Brushing my teeth was a chilling experiment in terror. I snagged the toothbrush in the stitches. My lip flared like a pit bull that had just been neutered without benefit of anesthetic.

After a breakfast of three aspirin and a Diet Pepsi, I put on a bathing suit, threw some clean clothes into a gym bag, and drove to the ocean.

Under the pink sky of dawn I went for a swim. The placid water was surprisingly warm for so early in the morning. I swam underwater in an irrational attempt to purge my system of all the unidentifiable emotional debris that was weighing me down. I was depressed, not really sure of the source. It could have been any number of things. I had been violated. My battered ego was sulking because I had been careless enough to get caught off guard. Someone had tried to scare me off. I scare easily. However, I do not scare off. I don't know who said it, it may have been me, but you cannot let fear govern your life. If you live it right, life is taking risks. I believe that. Unless it's personal. Then I play it safe.

I broke the surface of the water and began swimming away from the shore. One hundred yards. Two hundred yards. Maybe I was upset because I had seen Mali with another man and was afraid our friendship was in jeopardy. For every stroke I made gliding through the water, I could have added another possible reason. Which I knew was pointless.

I swam until my arms grew heavy and my legs could no longer kick. The point of no return had come and gone twice over. It was the farthest I had ever swum offshore. Not a water taxi in sight. As I treaded water under the cloudless sky, I began to wonder what I was doing. Trying to drown myself with a casual indifference? No, it wasn't that. Obviously, I was challenging myself. But to what end? I had to come up with a quick answer. I was tiring and would not be able to stay afloat much longer. I was forced to admit what I already knew. I was trying to restore my self-esteem. I was feeling the humiliation of victims of violence. That was the pill I had to swallow, bitter as it tasted. I had to accept that. At least it gave me something to focus on. Once I understand something, I can deal with it. Next, the trick was getting back to shore. I rolled on my back and began to float in with the current.

• • •

I took a long shower in the public bathhouse, entertaining the denizens with a muffled medley of the Righteous Brothers' greatest hits. I dressed in a pair of fresh jeans and my official private-investigator short-sleeved cotton shirt with a button-down collar. I slipped on a pair of boat shoes. I glanced at the big-lipped geek in the steamy mirror. If the lip got any larger I would have to name it. Set up a college fund for it.

I walked to the Sand Bar and made a pot of coffee. Too often I find myself asking, how come everybody knows that but me? Like, why didn't it occur to me that hot coffee was not the best thing in the world to pour over a freshly sutured wound in the mouth?

I called Nick Triandos. He picked up the receiver.

"Nick, it's me," I said. "Can you meet me at the Sand Bar?"

The line was quiet.

"This morning," I said.

There was a crunching sound.

"This antique gun thing, it looks like it's going to take both of us."

It sounded like Nick was chewing on burned toast.

"There's a new player in the game. A lady with a very sharp knife tried to persuade me to forget about the guns. She left her mark."

The line was quiet again.

"Nick?"

"Twenty minutes," he said, and hung up.

Carla came into the office as I was hanging up the phone. She was staring wide-eyed at my monster lip. A monster lip that would have frightened Kenneth Tobey and Richard Carlson right out of the B-movie business. Before Carla could ask her questions born of true concern, I stopped her with a humorless tone.

"Don't say a fucking word."

She gave me that look women give you when you tell them not to say a fucking word. Carla's only crime was that she cared about me and worried about me. If that wasn't a tear welling in her eye, it was certainly hurt. She walked out of the office.

She hadn't deserved that. I had unintentionally vented my frustration on an innocent bystander. I didn't know what to say to her. So I sat at my desk, feeling sorry for myself, having a grand time of it until a shadow fell over me. A thumb and an index finger the size of jumbo hot dogs clamped down on my swollen lip.

"Owwww!" It was the mother lode of pain, manna for a weight lifter.

Nick released his grip. "That's how you made Carla feel."

I pressed my hand over my throbbing mouth and nodded.

Nick sat down. "Start with the lip."

I told Nick about the long-legged acid-rock-queen-hitwoman. I told him about Eloise Loftus and her trifecta robberies. I told him about Wade Loftus and his little playmate. I told him what Sam said about the guns probably being overvalued.

Nick said, "Who hired the knife?"

I shrugged. "Wade Loftus did threaten me with his friends."

"We'll start with him."

I nodded. "I also want to ask his wife about the June twenty-sixth date. See if there's anything significant about that."

"I've got a question. Why did Wade Loftus wait two days before calling the police?"

"Let's go ask him."

• • •

The law offices receptionist stared at me. I looked familiar, but she couldn't place the lip.

"What hap—" She caught herself. "What can I do for you?" She was doing her best not to stare.

"Harry Rice and hired thug, here to put Wade Loftus through a psychological chamber of horrors," I said with a crazed look in my eyes. An exhibit of my bizarre sense of humor.

The receptionist smiled hesitantly, not sure what to make of the enormous Nick. "Do you have an appointment?" The programmed response, but it was delivered with a hint of amusement. I wasn't sure if that was because I looked like an MTV cartoon character or if the thought of Wade Loftus being put through a mind wringer pleased her.

Nick leaned over the desk. "Which calendar is his?"

The receptionist pushed an appointment book toward him. Nick glanced at the clock on the wall and then made an entry on the page.

He said, "We have an appointment."

The receptionist read the notation. "Ozzie and Harriet?"

Nick nodded. "I'm Ozzie."

She shrugged. "If you'll just have a seat. Mr. Loftus has someone with him at the moment. It should just be a minute. One of the other attorneys," she explained. "They can only stand each other for a few minutes at a time."

Nick and I sat in the waiting area. I picked up the morning newspaper on the coffee table and turned to the editorial page. Nick folded his arms and put on his game face. I only had time to check the Don Wright political cartoon when the door to Loftus's office swung open. A short, balding man with an angry face and an expensively tailored, gray pin-striped suit stormed out.

"You better do something about Tigertail." He was shouting. He turned back and pointed his finger at the open door. "I'm not going to put up with it much longer. This is your fault. You got us into this, now get us out."

He marched across the lobby and stopped at the receptionist's desk. "Any messages, Dottie?"

"Your wife called, Ira."

Ira glanced over at Nick. His eyes twinkled when he saw me. Beauty is in the eye of the beholder. Ira was beholding a potential malpractice suit.

He said something in a hushed voice to the receptionist.

She said, "They're waiting to see Wade."

The twinkling shark turned Gloomy Gus as he disappeared into another office.

The receptionist smiled. She did enjoy her job. She picked up the phone and punched a number. "Wade, your ten forty-nine appointment is here. Yes, I'm sure. Ozzie and Harriet." She cringed, then hung up the phone. She looked at Ozzie and said, "David and Ricky can't play today. But Wade will be right out."

"What the hell are you doing here!" Wade Loftus was standing in his doorway. Didn't seem at all pleased to see me.

"That him?" Nick asked me.

I nodded. "That him."

It was as if I had said Lights, camera, action. Nick was on his feet, charging Wade Loftus. That had to be a frightening sight. The attorney stood as motionless as an image in a freeze-framed video. Nick parked his mammoth hand on Loftus's chest and pushed the nervous lawyer back inside the office. I stood and slowly sauntered across the lobby.

"Hold all our calls," I said to the receptionist.

She batted her eyelashes. "Anything for you, Harriet."

I closed the door behind me. Nick had control of the situation. Wade Loftus was sitting in his swivel chair.

Nick was leaning over the chair, his hands on the armrests. Nick pushed his weight forward till Loftus was leaning back, looking at the ceiling.

Loftus looked at me as I walked into his line of vision. "Does he know I'm an attorney?" he said to me.

"He was trained on attorneys," I said. "You're probably wondering why I called this little confab."

"No, I wasn't wondering that," he said. "And I really don't care. I don't have time to see you now. I have to be somewhere else shortly. Now tell your friend to let me up."

Loftus would not look at Nick or speak to him.

"I wish I could help you there, Wade," I said. "He's bigger than me and usually doesn't do what I say. Maybe he'll listen to you. You're an attorney."

Loftus gave Nick his hostile witness stare. "Take your Neanderthal hands off my chair," he said, tight jawed. "If you don't let go immediately, I'll press charges against both of you for holding me hostage. Let go now!"

Nick smiled. He released his grip on the armrests while simultaneously kicking the wheels out from under the chair, somersaulting Wade Loftus to the floor. The chair followed and landed on top of him. Nick lifted the chair off and tossed it to the side. He hunkered next to the fallen Loftus.

Nick whispered, "Look at his lip."

"What?" said Loftus quietly, some of the starch knocked out of him.

"Look at his lip."

Loftus looked. He noticed it for the first time.

Nick said, "Not a pretty sight."

Nick locked his eyes on Loftus's so there would be no misunderstanding. Loftus understood. He was considerably shaken. The image he strove to maintain had collapsed. He was an educated man being confronted by one who didn't know about brains over brawn. Loftus glanced over at me.

"Look at me," Nick said. Loftus looked at Nick. "How did his lip get like that, Wade?"

Loftus looked at me and said, "What is this? How should I know? Weren't you there?"

There was sarcasm left in him.

"Talk to me." Nick's voice rumbled like a California earth tremor.

"I don't know how it happened. Let me up."

"Who did it?" Nick's voice had to be registering on the Richter scale. It unnerved me and he was on my side. God knows what it did to Wade Loftus.

"I don't know who did it." It sounded like Loftus was pleading for mercy. "Look, you can humiliate me. You can hurt me. It won't change anything."

"Who did you hire?" Nick said.

"No one."

"You threatened Harry with your friends."

"Christ! Is that what this is about? Let me up." Loftus struggled to sit up. Nick stiff-armed the attempt. "It was just talk. Big talk. That's all it was. I'm a lawyer. That's what lawyers do."

Nick looked at me.

"Let him up," I said.

He gave me a questioning look.

"I'm going to give him a little test, see if he's telling the truth."

Back on his feet, Wade Loftus was a big shot again. He picked up the phone on his desk. "Get out of my office now or I'm calling the police."

I sat down. Nick sat down. Loftus started to dial.

"Say, Wade, whatever happened to that little blond honey of yours?" I said casually.

Wade stopped dialing. "I don't know what you're talking about."

"Right. You don't know anything about any little blond mouse playing house while your wife was away. And you don't know anything about my lip."

"Now that's true. I didn't have anything to do with that."

"Or the blond?"

He put the phone down.

It took Wade Loftus about thirty minutes to tell his story. Take out the unnecessary details and it could have been told in five. But, not knowing how much I knew, Loftus was reluctant to leave anything out. It was the only way he could validate his claim that he was telling the truth and didn't know who had cut me.

Loftus said it started right after he dropped his wife off at the train station for her trip to Gainesville. He stopped at Fort Bush, a naked bar in Fort Lauderdale. He said he stopped on a lark, that he usually never went to those places except for an occasional bachelor's party. And he probably only chased ambulances to donate blood.

He said he had been sitting in Fort Bush having a few drinks. Probably wasn't even aware that naked women were swarming about. He said he had been there about twenty minutes when a scantily dressed blond came over and sat down next to him.

"Did you buy her a drink?" I said.

"Of course not. I know how that works."

"Tell us, Wade, how does that work?"

"The bartender gives the girl a glass of Seven-Up that's supposed to be champagne and you get charged seven dollars for it. Then the girl tells you to leave the bartender a three-dollar tip."

Nick said, "I'm working in the wrong bar."

Loftus said the blond introduced herself as "Lola." "I don't think that was her real name," he said.

"You're wise beyond your years," I said.

Loftus ignored me. He said he told Lola his name, and that she told him that he was different from most of the guys that came into Fort Bush.

"Lola ordered a drink," Loftus said. "The barmaid looked at me to see if it was okay. Lola said, 'No, Sherry, I'm buying my own drinks.' She said she just wanted to sit and talk to a decent guy. She said, 'I get tired of these animals that come in here. They think they can paw you and cop a feel just because they stuck a dollar in your garter. They'll leave me alone if they think I'm with you.' "

Loftus said it went that way until closing. After each of her dances, Lola would come back, sit next to him, and buy her own drink. At closing she went home with him.

The next morning, Loftus said, he invited Lola to spend the day with him. He called his office and found there were no pressing appointments, so he took the day off. By coincidence, Lola had the day off, too. She also had the next day off, but Loftus didn't. There was a professional seminar he had to attend. Still, he said, he invited Lola to spend the second day at the apartment, and she accepted. She asked Loftus if she could drive him to work. That way, she could use his car to go to the grocery store and make dinner for him. She even offered to pick him up after work. Loftus gave Lola the keys to Eloise's car instead of his.

That evening, when he returned home from work, he said, there was no dinner. No Lola. A cleaned out apartment. Eloise's car was parked in the garage and the keys were in the ignition.

"Why didn't you call the police then?" I said.

He looked at me as if I were of simian birth. "I couldn't. If I called the police and told them what happened, then Eloise would have found out about Lola. So I thought I would tell Eloise that I sold everything and had had the apartment redecorated as a surprise for her when she returned. But that wouldn't work either."

"Why not?"

"The guns," Nick said.

Loftus nodded. "I couldn't come up with enough cash to cover the alleged sale of the guns, in addition to everything else. If I charged all the new furniture she would want to know what had happened to the money from the sale of the guns. I couldn't tell the truth and I couldn't lie. So I decided to find Lola."

"And?"

"Nothing."

"What about Fort Bush?"

"They threw me out."

"You going to sue?"

"Give me a break."

"What did you do next?"

"I made the circuit of the strip bars in Broward and Dade counties, hoping she'd show up in one. I knew it was a long shot, but I didn't know what else to do. I talked to a lot of dancers, but they're a pretty protective union. Nobody knew her. Nobody knew anybody. So the only way to cover myself was to call the police, report a break-in, and collect the insurance."

"And leave out Lola."

"And leave out Lola," he parroted.

"What's Lola look like?"

"You're going to look for her?"

"Probably."

"She's about five feet tall. Bleached-blond hair."

"Platinum?"

"Yes. Sort of like Marilyn Monroe. Only Lola was bustier. Had full lips, almost like she was pouting."

"Anything else?"

He thought about something that made him smile. "A tattoo. She had a blue owl tattoo inside her thigh, just below her crotch."

"Did Lola seem particularly interested in your gun collection?"

"No. Just the opposite. She said guns frightened her."

"She didn't ask about their value, or you didn't brag about their worth?"

"No."

I looked at Nick. He nodded.

"All right, Wade. We believe you. Don't know that I'd hire you to defend me in a capital punishment case, but I believe you."

He was visibly relieved. "You going to tell Eloise?"

"No promises, but I don't know that it'll be necessary. She just wants the guns back. I don't think all this other stuff interests her."

"Anything else?" Loftus asked.

"Not now. Maybe later. Adios."

ten

·····

We stepped out of the air-conditioned law offices into the harsh glare of a midday sun.

"Did you believe him?" Nick said.

"You intimidated him. I think he was too scared to lie."

Nick considered that briefly. "Suppose he's covering for someone he's more afraid of."

"Covering for who? The hit woman?"

"Just thinking out loud."

Nick unlocked the doors of his Bronco. He climbed in behind the wheel. I got in the passenger side and said, "Drive down to the end of the block and park."

"No, thanks," Nick deadpanned. "You're not my type."

"There's good news."

Nick pulled out of the parking lot. He drove about thirty yards to the end of the street and parked in the shade of an oak tree so old that Fred Flintstone might have climbed it as a kid.

"Do I have time to grow sideburns?" Nick said, cutting off the ignition.

"You're in rare humor," I said. "You get laid this week?"

Nick grunted.

"Elvis has left the building."

"What?"

"Take a look," I said. I had been watching the law offices through the rearview mirror. Wade Loftus came out, carrying a package the size of three New York telephone books. "Follow him."

Loftus pulled out of the parking lot in a white Volvo. He turned in the opposite direction, and Nick did a quick U-turn.

The Volvo swung north on U.S. 1. Nick kept a couple cars between us and Loftus. We looped around Young Circle and headed west on Hollywood Boulevard, where downtown revitalization was apparent—brick sidewalks, planted palms, freshly painted pastel-colored buildings housing art galleries, the current-craze ethnic restaurants, retail stores specializing in everything from lace goods and Italian figurines to new furniture and used records. There was even a blues bar. The city had done a nice job. The once decaying street at least had hopes of restoring a bygone prosperity. It had everything but people. No customers. What's a city to do? If Hollywood was another small town dying slowly, at least it was going to look good in death.

I commented on the Bronco's pathetic shocks as we rattled over the railroad tracks that ran between the north- and southbound lanes of Old Dixie Highway. Nick ignored me.

Nick meandered skillfully through traffic, keeping the Volvo within reasonable distance. Not so close that Loftus could identify us and not so far away that Nick couldn't speed through a yellow light. Cruising through the circle that surrounds city hall, we inadvertently got too close when a beer truck changing lanes almost blindsided us. Nick had to accelerate to avoid a collision, and we got

close enough to the Volvo to read Loftus's vanity plate—
LAWYOUR Nick was able to cut behind a school van before
Wade could spot us.

At the Hollywood Boulevard and I-95 interchange,
Loftus turned onto the northbound entrance ramp. Traffic was backed up on the interstate. It had slowed to a
crawl. Nick switched on the car radio, which was tuned
to a country-western station. A nasal voice warbled a
lament about looking for a woman to ease the pain of
heartache brought on by another woman. The guy was a
goner.

We bumper-humped in the slow, moving traffic for almost thirty minutes before the bottleneck cleared. It had
been caused by a two-car accident.

The Wademobile stayed in the right-hand lane and
began to slow again as it approached the entrance ramp
to 595. Nick eased off the gas. The Volvo veered toward
the east as it climbed the entrance ramp. We went eastbound on the elevated highway that runs above the north
perimeter road of Fort Lauderdale–Hollywood International Airport. From that vantage is a good overall view
of the airport. Everything is in sight—runways, terminal
buildings, air cargo facilities, general aviation FBOs.

Highway 595 eastbound also empties into Port Everglades, and the traffic reflects that. Eighteen-wheelers
barreled past, spewing black smoke without regard for
the ecological consequences.

Loftus followed the trucks into Port Everglades. Nick
took cover behind a slow-moving panel truck. We drove
past a fuel farm and a container yard before Loftus turned
off on one of the side streets.

We dropped farther back. The Volvo pulled into a
crushed-shell parking lot of the port canteen. Nick backed
into the parking lot of a customshouse broker, which was
catercorner from the canteen. We had an unobstructed

view of Loftus's car. Conversely, he would have had one of us if he had bothered to look.

Loftus got out of his car. He glanced at his watch. He checked his reflection in the car window and toyed with his dark glasses. He fluffed his hair and got back in the car.

Nick said, "On surveillance with Nick and Nora."

"What happened to Ozzie and Harriet?"

"I don't look like an Ozzie."

"But I look like a—"

"Don't ask questions you don't want to hear the answers to," Nick interrupted.

A battered Dodge without a license plate drove by and pulled into the canteen parking lot. The driver got out of the car. He was dark-skinned and wearing an oily T-shirt and grease-covered work pants. The passenger door swung open, and out stepped a man with a pasty complexion. He was dressed the same as the driver.

The two men walked to the back of the Dodge and opened the trunk. At the same time, Wade Loftus got out of his car, carrying the package that he had left the law offices with. He walked to the rear of the Dodge, said something to the men, and then dropped the package into the open trunk.

The pale-looking one leaned over in the trunk. From where Nick and I were sitting it appeared that he was inspecting the contents of the package Loftus had deposited. The inspector stood up and closed the trunk. He nodded at the driver. The driver pulled an envelope from his back pocket and handed it to Loftus, who peered into it. He didn't seem pleased. Loftus said something to the driver. The driver said something to Loftus. Both of them started talking at the same time. The driver was getting animated, his arms flailing while his mouth jabbered on.

Loftus backhanded the driver across the face, and

everything became still. No one was speaking. Finally Loftus pointed a finger at the driver's face and said something, then turned and stared at the other man, who just grinned and shrugged. Loftus got into his car and drove away.

The two men watched Loftus drive off. The driver said something that made his partner laugh. They walked into the canteen.

"Strange," I said.

"What the hell was that all about?"

"I'd like to know that myself. What would Loftus be selling to crew members? Certainly not drugs. That's what the crew would sell."

Nick said, "Want to follow him?"

"No. Let's go back to the Sand Bar. I owe Carla an apology."

eleven

·········

A Poem for Carla

BY RALPH WALDO RICE

The lip from the black lagoon
Had a habit of speaking too soon.
Rather than follow the fine print of the heart,
It would blurt things that weren't very smart.
Though spoken words cannot be taken back,
I surely hope you can cut me some slack.
If you don't, this poem could run all day,
When "Carla, I'm sorry" is all I wanted to say.

• • •

Carla folded the slip of paper and looked at me.

I said, "Are we okay?"

A little smile spread on her lips. "Maybe." She stood up. "I've got to get back to work."

"Nick's got the bar covered."

"It's my shift." She slipped the piece of paper into her jeans pocket.

"Wait a minute. You can't take that with you. I don't want anybody else to see it."

"Then watch your mouth and you won't have anything to worry about. But if you ever talk to me like that again, I'll photocopy this and spread it all over the beach."

"Carla, that's not fair. The crime doesn't fit the punishment."

"That's not my problem, pal."

She walked out of my office.

The moral of the story: Never apologize to a woman in writing.

I followed her into the bar.

Nick was serving drinks to a couple of old men dressed in faded dark suits with lapel carnations. Two on-call pallbearers waiting for work, and feeding time with stories about who they had outlived. I wandered behind the bar and pulled a can of Sprite from the cooler.

"Guy at the table next to the window was asking to see you," Nick said over my shoulder.

I glanced at the table. I was being stared at by someone too old to own any New Kids on the Block records and too young for midlife crisis. He had thin blond hair and would be bald by the time he was forty. He wore one of those shirts with an alligator on it. There was something familiar about him.

I walked over to him and said, "I'm supposed to know you, aren't I?"

"Sit down, please." He had a deep, low voice, one you'd expect from a man twice his size. I knew I had heard it before. I sat across from him. He squinted. "Your lip."

"Oh, how nice of you to notice."

A mechanical smile. He extended his hand. "Milton Brantferger. I worked for you one summer. Seven years ago. Right after I got out of college."

We shook. "I remember."

"I had a beard. More hair."

"I remember already. Did I pay you?"

"Minimum wage. Invaluable experience. It helped me qualify for the state private investigator's license."

"Okay," I said.

There was an undisguised awkward silence.

I said, "Are you looking for work?"

"No. No, I'm working. In fact, I'm working right now."

"What? Something you need my help with?"

"Possibly. Let me tell you what I'm working on." He flipped open a little spiral pad that had been lying on the table unnoticed by me. He read from his notes: "This morning at sunrise you went for a swim in the ocean. After that you cleaned up and came here, to the Sand Bar. At ten-twenty you and that big fellow over there left here. You drove to some law offices on Washington Street. At noon you came out, drove to the end of the block, and waited. Less than a minute later someone came out of the building and drove off in a white Volvo, which you followed."

"Did you get the license plate?"

"Yes. Do you want it?"

"No."

"Do you want me to tell you what happened in Port Everglades?"

"What's going on? You following me?"

Milton Brantferger said yes.

I said, "Why are you telling me this?"

"Professional courtesy."

"What's my second choice?"

He reached into his pocket and pulled out some bills.

He laid the money on the table. "Five hundred dollars. I don't have time to be following you. I have other cases to be working. However, I never turn down a job. Those I don't have time to do personally, I farm out."

"You're hiring me to follow me?"

"In essence, yes. I was hired to follow you for five days. Today's half over. It'd be a lot easier for me, and more profitable for you, if you would just call me at the end of the day and tell me where you've been. I don't need to know who you were talking to, or what about. I was hired simply to find out where you went. You tell me, I tell my client, and nobody will be the wiser."

"I'm impressed, Milton. Did I teach you this?"

"No."

"Suppose I go someplace I don't want you to know about. Am I allowed to lose you?"

He shook his head. "I get top dollar because I'm good. Besides, you're not even aware that you're being followed."

"Well, I wasn't, that's true."

"Were you planning to go someplace you don't want me to know about?"

I thought about that and couldn't think of anyplace.

Milton said, "Here's my phone number. If I'm not in, just leave the information on the answering machine."

"Five days, huh?"

"Five phone calls. Five hundred dollars."

"I like the way you do business, Milton."

He stood up to leave. "You didn't ask who hired me."

I stood up. "I didn't ask how much you got paid to tail me."

The mechanical smile again. "You don't want to know."

He walked out.

My first thought was that someone wanted to make

sure I had taken last night's professional discouragement seriously. My second thought was, what next?

"Harry, you have a call." Carla held up the phone.

I scooped the money off the table and went to the bar.

Carla held her hand over the mouthpiece. "I forgot to tell you earlier. While you and Nick were out, Mali called. She said to tell you she was going to be out of town for a few days and would call you when she got back."

I nodded, reached across the bar, and took the phone. "Hello."

"Hi, Harry. It's Eloise Loftus. Are you busy?"

I hesitated. "I don't think so."

"Can we meet someplace?"

"I suppose. Sure."

"I mean now. Someplace where I can get a drink."

"You want to come here?"

"No. Someplace else."

"Okay. What's up?"

"Wade just called me. He told me you had been to visit him this morning. He told me . . . He told me all of it, Harry."

"What's 'all of it'?"

There was a protracted silence before she said in a small voice, "Lola."

twelve

•••••••••

Sara's is an old neighborhood bar just beyond social concern. Cast in the shadows of poor lighting, it resembles a barroom set from a 1940s low budget, black-and-white Foreign Legion serial. Just dark enough so a lip shaped like a carnival ride can enter unnoticed. Beer is the specialty of the house. Bottles, cans, and just about everything but dog spit on tap. No wine spritzers or coolers. No pink drinks with umbrellas. No crystal clear malts that taste like Karo syrup. A place where people who have fallen from grace can excuse themselves from rejection and seek the tenderness of a motel romance with the trailer park whore. Sara's is not listed in any of the tourist guidebooks.

There were a few empty spaces at the far end of the bar. I walked past an assorted collection of visionaries and dreamers sharing their ambitions and goals with anyone who would listen, or not. I plopped onto the last stool.

The bartender wore a brown terry cloth bathrobe. She stalked back and forth behind the bar like the referee in a morality tag-team match between saints and sinners. As far as I was concerned she was a saint.

Her name was Ellen Matonis. She was a sixty-year-old reformed drug addict. She had a heart of lead and didn't take crap from anyone. After Theresa died I would have drunk myself to death if hadn't been for Ellen Matonis. It's a long story, but that's the end of it.

Ellen gazed impassively at my mouth. "If that's your look of love you're going to die a horny man, Harry."

"Then I'll die as I lived."

Ellen snorted, which is how she laughs.

I ordered a bottle of beer and a bag of potato chips. Except for the three aspirins to start the morning, I hadn't put anything solid in my stomach all day.

By the time Eloise Loftus arrived, I had finished half the beer and discarded the chips after the first taste of salt hit the lip. Standing in the open doorway, dressed in her teaching threads, she was as out of place in Sara's as the bar shuffleboard machine would have been in an operating room. Eloise spotted me just as I started to wave to her. While she made her way down the bar, I picked up my beer and chivalrously moved to one of the cable-spool tables. It struck me that she was not the type to sit at a bar. I'm sensitive to that kind of thing. Sometimes a little late, but eventually I get it.

She was still absorbing the ambiance as she sat down. "This is the last time I let you pick the place."

"I thought you might be more comfortable in a place where you wouldn't be recognized."

"There are many places I wouldn't be recog—" She saw The Lip. "Harry." Her voice became soothing. She placed her open hand against my cheek. "What happened?"

"I was teaching Hebrew to ghetto kids when five of them pulled knives on me. It was my own fault. I shouldn't have told them that I wasn't grading on a curve."

Eloise gave me an oddly distant look. "I don't need jokes right now, Harry."

No she didn't. It had to be tough for her—discovering that her husband had been playing pickup games in the Junior Miss League. She had just learned that fidelity was just another word for no one else to do.

I said, "On the phone you said you wanted a drink."

She nodded. "I do. It's a shame drinks don't cure everything."

"That's where I come in. What drink can't drown, I fix."

Her eyes narrowed. "I hope that's true."

"What are you drinking?"

"A beer will be fine."

I went to the bar.

Over beers, Eloise told me that Loftus was her second husband. Her first marriage had a fourteen-year run. It ended in divorce nine years ago. There was a daughter, who stayed with the father. Eloise hadn't seen her ex-husband since the divorce. She hadn't seen her daughter since marrying Wade, five years ago. She told me all of this without emotion.

As it neared happy hour Sara's began to fill. Muffled background voices became louder. Boisterous laughter from the bar inhibited conversation.

"Could we go to your place?" Eloise said.

I looked questioningly at her. I knew she wasn't talking about the Sand Bar.

"I could fix us something to eat," she said.

"There's no food there."

"It doesn't matter."

"Let me pay the bill."

Ellen watched Eloise leave the building as I settled the tab.

"New lady?" Ellen said.

"A client."

"Watch out for that one, Harry."

"Thank you, Miss Lonely Hearts."

We left my car at Sara's. I gave Eloise the directions to my house and we rode in relative silence. The lack of sleep the night before and the beers on an empty stomach were beginning to catch up with me. I was bone tired.

Eloise parked in my driveway. She cut the engine and turned to me. "Wade told me that the burglary occurred two days before he reported it. June twenty-sixth. That's my daughter's birthday."

I faced her. "All right. If you want to talk shop, I say there's a definite pattern. Lola, or someone using her, set up Wade. Your anniversary, his birthday, and your daughter's birthday. I don't believe in that kind of coincidence."

"You think someone is after him?"

"It would appear that way."

"Then why my car and my office?"

"Opportunity. When Wade let Lola borrow your car—"

"He didn't tell me that."

"—he gave her your key ring. I assume your house, office, and car keys were all on it."

"Yes. She had copies made, then."

"If she had used Wade's car, then it probably would have been his car that was stolen and his office that was hit."

"How could they have planned on Wade going to the bar?"

"I don't know that they could. Maybe the plan just formulated ad hoc. I'm not sure about that."

"But why continue? What are they after? They stole everything that was in the apartment. Why go on?"

"I don't know."

"Do you think Lola knows?"

"She's a lead," I said. "I don't think she was acting alone. She couldn't have emptied your apartment without help. There's something else you should know. My lip was cut last night by a knife-wielding woman. She told me to forget about the gun collection."

The shock on Eloise's face was real. "Who? Why?"

"That's what I'm asking you."

"You think I had something to do with that?"

"No. But is there something about that gun collection you haven't told me?"

"I swear to God, I can't imagine anything that . . . Harry, I don't know anything about this. Do you think Wade does?"

"That's why I went to see him this morning."

"And?"

"He says he doesn't know anything."

She nodded. "It's not his style. He wouldn't know how to arrange something like that." She turned away and stared out the window. When she looked back at me her eyes were serious. "Can we go inside?"

I didn't answer right away, because I knew the scenario too well. She would seek what her husband had taken from her: an affirmation that she was still a desirable woman. I would use her to lock on to reminiscences of lost feelings. To an outsider we would look like two cheerless papier-mâché figures sitting on the periphery, waiting for a streetcar without a name or destination. She would be tentative. I would be clumsy. There would be long periods of uneasy silence. She would extend her muted desires, which I would humbly accept. Eventually, she would ask me if I wanted to make love. Of course I wanted to make love, but I could only do that with a woman I loved. What would I do if she asked if I wanted to screw?

It was that presumption of sequence that made me realize I did have a preference. I didn't want to do this. The damn thing about it was, I found Eloise Loftus a most desirable woman. So what was my problem? Was it Wade Loftus? Was I having pangs of conscience for having bullied him in his office, and balling his wife would just increase my self-disapproval? Probably not.

I can rationalize most of my actions. Why, to hear me pontificate, you'd half expect to see me on TV hawking Saint Harry's Holier-Than-Thou Seminar in Decency. Talk about sidestepping the truth.

The fact was, the assault on Wade Loftus wasn't necessitated by the search for truth, justice, and the American Way. It was the cheap shot of a competing suitor. I am not a paragon of virtue, but I did plot my own moral map. I wish I didn't stray from it.

I let her come in.

She followed me up the porch steps and stood behind me as I unlocked the door. Inside, she asked for the bathroom. I pointed down the hall, avoiding her eyes. She went that way; I went to the kitchen. I pulled a beer from the refrigerator.

In the living room I slumped into an overstuffed chair.

Eloise walked into the room. Her makeup was fresh. It looked as if she had spent only enough time on her short dark hair to run her fingers through it. Any more time and effort would have ruined the effect. With a nervous smile she asked to use my phone. I pointed to the kitchen.

I waited silently, sipping my beer.

She carried a beer when she returned from the kitchen. It was for me. I had drunk just enough to take the edge off but not enough to stop. She sat on the floor, resting her arm and head on my leg, increasing the tension in my groin. I caressed her forehead with my fingertips. She looked up at me. I sat the beer on the floor. She squeezed my leg and slowly eased up until she was sitting on my lap. She leaned forward and gingerly planted a kiss on my wounded lip. I squirmed. She pressed against my rising member. Soon we were touching in a way that forever changes the relationship between a man and a woman. Strangers no more. It happened before I was even aware that my hand was cupped over the bare flesh of her breast.

I pulled back. I stared at her taut nipples. I wanted to take them in my mouth. Instead, and reluctantly, I started buttoning her blouse.

Her moist eyes asked the question.

I said, "I can't. I'd be using you. I don't want to do that."

"What do you think I'm doing to you? Two consenting adults. Nothing more. No expectations."

"I'm not consenting." What was I suppose to say to her? I know my feelings, I just don't know how to express them? I don't like the idea of using another sentient being as a sperm depository? I've had better, I know what it's like to be held by someone you care about?

"There are worse ways of being used."

"Users are users," I said. "There's no satisfaction for me in that."

She ground her hip into my erection.

"I didn't say it didn't hurt."

The phone rang. Whoever was calling, I owed them.

"I better get that."

She studied my face without any sense of urgency.

The phone rang.

Satisfied with what she saw, she got up.

The phone rang.

"Hello."

"Peter Gunn?"

The voice didn't register. My brain was still waiting for my lower region to return some blood to it.

"Harry? You there?"

"Yes."

"You still looking for the guns?"

"Sam. I'm sorry. I didn't recognize your voice."

"You sound out of it. Did I wake you or something?"

"Or something."

"You sound it. Maybe you could use some good news."

"I'm not sure I'd know good news if I heard it. What do you have?"

"A lead. I've located one of the Lugers from the Loftus collection."

"Positive?"

"Serial number matches."

"How did you find it?"

"Confidential information, my friend."

"It doesn't matter. Where's the gun?"

"A pawnshop in Medley."

"Will they talk to me?"

"Tell 'em Sam sent you."

"Got an address?"

"Got a pencil?"

I jotted down the information and thanked Sam. He said he had a few more leads he was working and would let me know if anything materialized.

I hung up. Eloise was standing in the doorway, her clothing fixed.

I said, "I have a lead on one of the guns. You still want me to pursue this?"

"Yes," she whispered.

"Listen, Eloise, I'm coming off a sleepless night—"

She held up a hand. "It's okay. I'll drive you back to your car."

As we walked across the yard toward her car, she stuck her arm in mine and squeezed. She opened the passenger door for me and kissed my cheek before letting go of my arm. Show time for the neighborhood-watchers.

Eloise dropped me off at Sara's. I went in and had a few more beers I didn't need or really want. When I finally got home I called Milton Brantferger. I got a recording. I gave my evening's itinerary and hung up. I flopped on the couch and fell asleep watching a 1938 Loretta Young movie. An old Burns and Allen show was on when I woke up. It was after midnight. I watched the rest of George and Gracie's program, not really concentrating. My mind kept flipping back through the pages of the past few days. It didn't make for peaceful reading. Say good night, Gracie.

thirteen

· · · · · · · · · ·

In the morning I awakened with the face of a headliner in a sideshow: Freaks International presents Quasimodo Mouth, appearing nightly on stage with Fat Feet Frank; the incredible Snake Dick—every woman's dream; Chicken Dog, the feathered canine; and the world-famous Princess Humongoustits.

As horrible as the lip looked, the stomach felt worse. It was as if it hadn't been fed since DC Comics were a dime. Small wonder, following a day bereft of nutrition but for half a potato chip and a wholesome dose of beer.

I walked downtown to Minnie's Good Guys Diner and was greeted by the vacuous smile of a painted-faced waitress. We admired each other's masks and then I ordered breakfast. I swilled a pint of orange juice and a bucket of coffee before shoveling in a mound of scrambled eggs and a pile of potatoes and onions. I began to feel better than I looked.

● ● ●

Medley is an industrial section in west Dade County. The pawnshop Sam told me about was on South River Drive, an access road that parallels U.S. 27, a.k.a. Okeechobee Road. The roads are separated by a canal, or a river, depending on how generous the definition. Hence, South River Drive is mostly local traffic. Route 27 is filled with pickup trucks towing airboats, dump trucks spraying dust by the acre, semis ignoring the speed limit, ptomaine lunch wagons and minivans carrying tourists who don't know the better routes.

The pawnshop was in a converted two-story wood-frame house surrounded by scrub. I parked on a bed of pine needles. The front window was filled with hocked musician's dreams—trombones, trumpets, saxophones, guitars, keyboards, drums, harmonicas—and the usual array of watches and Instamatics.

The front door was unlocked, which was not typical of Dade County pawnshops. Most have locked doors and iron-barred windows. To get in, a customer has to ring a bell and wait to be buzzed in.

The place smelled as foul as an insurance salesman's promise. There was no one in the front room. A scrambling sound came from behind the counter. Then I saw the security guard waddle into view, an overweight rottweiler with a head the size of a Volkswagen. It was more intimidating than any gun-toting Wackenhut maniac. The dog ambled toward me with stringy saliva festooned around its gaping lower jaw.

I took a step back. Yeah, don't let the dog know you're scared.

"Don't be afraid of Oprah. About the only thing you have to worry about is, she might lick you to death." So wheezed an enormous man with a yellow smile. If fat was an Olympic event, this guy was a gold medal winner. The sleeves on his shirt were the size of tennis skirts. He had entered through French doors which led to what once might have been the dining room. The walk left him out of breath. "Sit, Oprah."

Oprah sat. Good, Oprah.

The fat man looked me over curiously, as if I were wearing wax Halloween lips.

"You buying or selling?" he gasped.

"Neither. Sam sent me."

He nodded. "You Harry Rice?"

"What's left of him."

His head continued to bob. "You're buying. You don't have a watch. Give you a nice timepiece. Fifty bucks."

"I don't have a watch because I don't want a watch."

He considered that. Apparently the price was negotiable.

"You have a trombone?"

"No."

"I got one you can have for forty dollars. Comes with its own carrying case."

"I know where I can get one for twenty-five dollars."

"Yeah," he hacked, "and it'll sound like a twenty-five dollar horn, too. For twenty-five dollars you can't be too sure of what you're buying. Cheap horns don't always blow true."

"What do thirty-five-dollar horns sound like?"

The yellow grin grew wide enough for the Munchkins to dance on. "For thirty-five dollars you can be sure of what you're buying."

I was the proud owner of a 1958 trombone. I didn't have to buy lessons. I paid him. He told me to take the trombone in the case held together by twine out of the front window. I took it out of principle and as a gift for Nick.

I was invited into the back. Oprah looked up at me and wagged her stump as I walked past her. I followed the fat man into the back room, where he settled into a recliner. He pushed back, elevating his legs.

"Got to keep my feet up," he said. "Bad circulation."

I sat on a wicker tub chair.

The fat man took a deep breath and said, "What's your interest in the gun?"

"It's part of a stolen gun collection. I was asked to recover the guns."

"That's what you do? Look for stuff people say is stolen?"

"Sometimes."

"Fool's errands," he deciphered.

I shrugged. "It can be. It has been."

We stared at each other for a moment.

"Want to see the gun?" he said suddenly.

I said I did.

"In the table drawer behind you."

There was a library table against the wall. I took the gun out of the drawer. It was a 9mm double-action Luger, sealed in a plastic bag. I checked the serial number with the list Eloise had given me. A match.

I said, "Is the trombone I bought stolen, too?"

"You got a smart mouth," he snapped angrily.

"This gun was stolen."

"That gun was reported stolen. There's a big difference."

I looked at him. That little outburst had left him breathless. He pointed to a bookcase. "Give me that ledger. January–March quarter. Second-to-top shelf."

I handed the bile green volume to him. He leafed through the pages. It took him about thirty seconds to find what he was looking for.

"When was the gun supposed to have been stolen?" he whispered.

I said, "The end of June."

He pointed to an entry. "Take a look. I bought the gun March eighteenth. Three months before it was reported stolen."

I looked at the page. On March 18 the fat man had paid four hundred dollars cash to a Mr. W. Landau. No address.

"What's the gun worth?" I asked.

"Eight hundred. Might get a thousand from a beginning collector who doesn't know better."

"You remember the guy you bought it from?"

He nodded. "Tall. About your age. Had a permanent. Don't know what's happening to men these days. Dressed like he didn't need the money. One of them Yuckies."

"Did he say why he was selling?"

"He didn't say. I didn't ask."

"Did you check his identification?"

"What for? You know how easy it is in Florida to get an ID with any name on it? No point in looking. I did check the serial number to see if it was hot. It wasn't. We agreed on price. End of business."

"You said tall."

"Like a basketball player."

"And he dressed like . . ."

"A professional. Coat and tie. Like a banker or a stockbroker."

"Or a lawyer?"

"Sure."

Tall like a basketball player. Styled hair. Dressed like a lawyer. W. Landau. W.L. I wondered if Wade Loftus knew anyone like that. Like "Mirror, mirror on the wall . . ."

fourteen

· · · · · · · · · · ·

I was the only person on the beach that day carrying a trombone.

No bikini-clad teenyboppers tagged along after me. It seemed that, unlike rock stars and lifeguards, trombonists did not have groupies. I never knew that.

Two young men, who could have been cover models for *Steroid Studs,* were sitting at the bar flirting with Carla. They wore wedgie briefs and tank tops cut off just below the rib cage, exposing washboard stomachs. They were lean, solid, tan, and pretty, and they came on to Carla with the confidence of men who had escaped the torture rack of rejection. I knew the type. Their glands were always in overdrive. When they masturbated it wasn't for self-gratification as much as it was out of self-devotion. It was a safe bet that they had never read a book; could name at least two NFL teams; went to singles bars and drank androgen on the rocks; didn't know what philosophical differences were; thought Beirut was a new yogurt flavor; knew more about horseplay than they knew about foreplay; and yet, could still have any woman they wanted. In short, they were everything I wanted to be.

Al and Irma and Father Shifty were sitting at one of the tables.

Seeing me, Al seized the moment. "You owe me a round, Harry," he called.

I held out the trombone case and said, "Would you settle for a little Jack Teagarden instead?"

"Harry, get over here!" Irma snapped, surprising Al, Shifty, and me. She was normally very soft-spoken.

Al looked up at me. "Sounds to me like you better get your ass over here."

"What?" I said. "She doesn't like Teagarden?"

When I got close enough to the table, Irma grabbed my wrist and pulled me down onto the chair between her and Shifty. With one hand she pushed back my forehead. The other hand gently lifted my lip. Irma examined my stitches. Even I hadn't had the stomach to do that.

"Oh, honey," she said mournfully. "What have you gotten into?" Her eyes explored my face, searching for signs of intelligent life. She shook her head. "I swear. You require more coddling than my own boys did when they were children."

Al said, "How's he supposed to tell you what happened while you're holding his lip up like that?"

"He can't order that round he owes us either," said Shifty.

Irma let go of my face. "Does it hurt?"

Al sighed. "Jesus, Irma. Are you writing a book?"

She looked at her husband. "Yes," she said defiantly.

"Well, leave that chapter out. 'Does it hurt?' What the hell kind of question is that?"

"Alcohol is good for pain," Dr. Father Shifty prescribed.

"For God's sake," Irma mumbled.

Time to steer the conversation in another direction

before I got caught in the crossfire of marital strife and religious fervor.

"So does anybody want to see my trombone?" I said.

There were no takers, to my disappointment. I kind of wanted to see what I had bought. For all I knew I'd been hauling around an empty trombone case. Or it might have contained the very instrument Al Capone played in his junior-high-school band. Wait. Call Geraldo.

"Harry, can I see you over here for a second." Carla beckoned from behind the bar. Geraldo would have to make do for a while longer with interviewing teachers who didn't wear underpants.

As I excused myself from the table, Irma grabbed my hand.

"Be careful," she ordered.

I leaned over and pecked her on the lips. She squeezed my hand and let go. With trombone tucked under arm I sidled over to the bar.

"Carla, send a round of drinks over to Al's table," I said. "Put it on my tab."

She said, "Add the usual forty percent tip?"

"Gee, Carla, what's forty percent of gratis?"

She did a quick calculation. "Twenty-three dollars. New math," she explained. "You're too old to have been taught it in school, Harry."

"Good, that makes this an old math bar. Now what was it you wanted to see me about?"

Carla stuck out her lower lip in a mock pout—or was she making fun of my lip mutation? She gestured with her head. "That guy over there in the blue shirt wants to see you."

I looked in the direction of a man in a light blue *guayabera*. He had a long face and dull brown eyes. His hair was shiny black and combed straight back like a Latin matinee idol's. Gold encircled his neck, his wrists, and most of his fingers. I caught him looking at us, and then he approached me.

"Mr. Rice?" he said.

"That's right."

"My employer would like to meet with you to discuss a matter of some interest to you." Just a flea's breath of a Spanish accent. He had probably moved to Miami from Havana when he was a kid. It was that slight an accent.

"Yeah? What interests me?"

"I'm told a certain gun collection."

"All right. Tell your employer I'm interested in meeting with him. Tell him he can stop by or he can call and make an appointment."

"Actually, he has requested that I escort you to his home," he said almost apologetically.

"He has, has he? And just who might your employer be?"

"My employer will make his own introductions. If it is acceptable to you, I have a car—"

"I get carsick."

"—and I will drive you there, and when my employer has finished conducting his business with you, I will drive you back here, or wherever you wish to be dropped off."

"That's damn sweet of you. What if circumstances force me to decline your employer's most gracious invitation?"

"Well, that would be most unfortunate." His voice was earnest.

"Your employer would undoubtedly dock your pay." I tried to sound sympathetic.

"No," he corrected with a mischievous grin. "I did not mean it would be unfortunate for my employer or myself."

"Why, shucks, that just leaves me then."

"Yes."

"I guess that means you would try to convince me to alter my plans and comply with your employer's invitation."

He nodded solemnly. "I can be very persuasive."

"Not too heavy on the humility, now."

"I'm parked on Johnson Street."

I persuade easy. I placed the trombone case on the bar.

"Carla," I said, "give this to Nick when he comes in. Tell him it's a clue."

Carla said, "I don't get it."

"That's all right. Nick won't either. I'll be back in . . ."

I looked at Blue Shirt. He shrugged. "I'll be back whenever."

"Everything all right, Harry?" She sounded concerned.

"Everything is fine. I'll be brunching with the Hoffas." I turned to my escort and said, "Let's go for a ride."

• • •

We rode in style—a white 1957 Cadillac in showroom condition. It was a straight shot down A1A through Hallandale and Haulover Beach to an oceanfront high-rise in Bal Harbour.

The doormen were dressed better than the queen's honor guard. They certainly were dressed better than me.

The penthouse elevator reminded me of the lobby of the Biltmore Hotel in Coral Gables. Blue Shirt pushed a combination panel for the nonstop ride up to the economic stratosphere. From the limited facts before me, I concluded that Blue Shirt's employer had money.

The elevator doors opened to an antechamber fit for a bishop. A life-size statue of the Virgin Mother stood on a pedestal in the center of the circular room. On the walls were paintings depicting the stations of the cross. The floor was Italian marble. Above the elevator door a security camera was panning the room. Love thy neighbor doesn't necessarily mean you have to trust the bastard. Somewhere on the other side of the ten-foot-high mahogany doors there had to be one very rich, paranoid Catholic.

Behind the double doors was a long corridor. We turned at the first door on the right, into a room completely devoid of religion or mercy. It was a gym, well stocked with Nautilus equipment and free weights. All four walls were mirrored. Working out in a corner was a short, stocky man with muscular shoulders and a neck like a bulldog's. I would have put him between sixty and seventy years old. He wore baggy boxer gym shorts, sweat socks, and black high-top sneakers. He was holding a barbell loaded with weights, doing shoulder shrugs. Through the looking glass we exchanged nods. I heard the door close behind me. I turned. Blue Shirt was gone. The old weight lifter put down the barbell and picked up a towel.

As he wiped the perspiration from his head, he said, "Good of you to come." Heavy on the Spanish accent.

"Silly me. I thought attendance was mandatory."

He lowered the towel and ran his eyes over me like an auctioneer appraising a side of beef. He looked familiar, like a page from yesteryear's newspaper.

"Mandatory may be too strong a word," my host said. "I would prefer to think that attendance was strongly recommended."

A movement across the room caught my eye. She was sitting on a bench, resting her arms upright on her legs with a dumbbell in each hand. She was doing wrist curls.

The old man said, "I believe you have already met Carmen."

I had. Only this time she wasn't dressed in black leather or flashing steel in my face. She wore a pink leotard.

Carmen dropped the dumbbells on the floor mat. She brushed a mass of dark curls from her face.

She smiled. "Nice to see you again, Harry."

"Is it?"

"I'm glad you are okay."

"Nothing personal, right? The things we do for our daily bread?"

She shrugged and said to the old man, "Do you want me to stay, Mundo?"

Mundo! Headlines from yesteryear all right. This was Mundo Cruz. A many times indicted and occasionally convicted career bad man. Mundo Cruz used to make Ming the Merciless seem like a Salvation Army Santa Claus.

"Go, Carmen," Mundo said. "Harry and I can settle this matter between us. You agree, Harry?"

There were few, if any, people alive who had disagreed with Mundo Cruz. I did not want to tangle with him. Legend had it that at fourteen Cruz shot off the leg of a man who had kicked Mundo's dog.

I said, "Whatever the matter is, it can be settled, Mr. Cruz."

Carmen left without stabbing me.

Mundo Cruz turned to me. "You know who I am." It was not a question.

"I know who you were."

"You thought I was dead."

"Dead may be too strong a word."

He politely ignored my anxiety-caused faux pas. "Not dead. Just retired."

"I hope to retire someday."

That made him smile. "Yes, I'm sure. I sense we have

an understanding already. That is good. That will make our business easier, you think?"

"Well, just what business is that?"

"I would prefer to ask the questions."

"By all means. I insist."

Cruz nodded, accustomed to having his way. "You are looking for a gun collection." Again, not a question. "What is your interest?"

"Money."

"How much?"

"Possibly as much as ten thousand dollars."

He looked at me evenly. "You seem a sensible man. I am surprised for so little money you would risk your life."

"No," I corrected. "I risk my life for no amount of money."

"No? Yet you did not take Carmen's warning seriously."

"I thought she was joking," I said in spite of myself.

Cruz's expression became grim. "And me? You think I'm a joker, too?"

"No." I bit my tongue. I almost told Cruz he was anything but a joker.

Cruz was staring at me, perhaps wondering what size cement shoe I wore. He started to towel-dry his arms. "You have a client?" he said.

"No one I'm loyal to," I answered. Lest he think I was joking again I added, "Let me explain that. I haven't been hired by anyone. A sort of bounty has been placed on the guns. I collect only if I recover and return the collection. I'm sure anyone could get the same deal."

"From Mrs. Loftus?"

"You don't need me to tell you that."

Cruz began to pat down his legs with the towel. "Would you lose interest in the guns for two thousand dollars?" he said.

"At one time I might have considered it. However, that was before some unexpected medical expenses."

Cruz gazed up at my lip. "Perhaps that is my fault," he conceded. "Sometimes I forget that the old ways are not always the best ways." He paused. "I pay for my mistakes. Five thousand dollars and you do it my way."

It sounded to me like I had bargaining power. "I do it your way and I stand to lose five thousand dollars. I can make ten thousand if I find the gun collection."

"This is true," Cruz said. "But if you do it my way, you do not get cut again."

"I like your way," I said. "Just what way is that?"

Mundo Cruz dried his torso as he studied me. He slipped on a sweatshirt and mounted an Exercycle. He pedaled slowly, examining me. There appeared to be an unspoken agreement between us. Cruz would talk when he was ready, and I wouldn't. The roles were clearly defined. One ventriloquist and one dummy. We each knew our part.

Cruz looked past me. He stopped pedaling. Someone had entered the room.

"Come in, Luis," Cruz said.

Luis, of the blue *guayabera,* was carrying a thick envelope. He handed it to Cruz.

Cruz removed a stack of hundred-dollar bills. He counted out fifty bills and put the rest back in the envelope. He held the cash out for me to take. We exchanged glances. This was the contract. If I took the money I was accepting his terms, his payoff to forget about the guns. It was the first offer I had ever had to sell out.

I took it.

fifteen

· · · · · · · · ·

The Friday happy hour crowd was spilling over onto the Broadwalk. Day-shift waitresses with swollen ankles and off-duty gelato servers still in uniforms skimpier than the Dolphin cheerleaders' were vying for bar stools with the hopes of positioning themselves next to a man they would have more in common with than just mutual contempt.

Nick and Carla both were working the bar and the floor. Nilsson sang Fred Neil on the jukebox.

I made my way through a trio of young women wearing more suntan oil than clothes. It was a tight, but memorable, squeeze. By the time I reached the office I smelled of cocoa butter.

There was a message on my desk that Sam Maturano had called. I dialed his number.

"Old Stuff," he answered.

"What's new?" I said.

"Everything but your stale joke."

Sam told me that he had appraised the gun collection, using several buyer's guides. He asked me if I remembered what he had said about condition. I said condition was the primary factor. He told me that without seeing the guns, and assuming all were in excellent condition, the best estimate he could come up with was thirty thousand dollars. He also told me that that was a liberal estimate. I told Sam I appreciated the information and his time. I did not tell him I was no longer interested in the guns. Sam said, wait, there's something else.

"I've located two more guns from the collection," he said. "The JoLo-Ar nine millimeter and one of the Walther Lugers. A collector in Boca Raton has them. The strange thing is, Harry—"

"I know. The guns were bought before they were reported stolen."

"Two weeks before. How'd you know?"

"I'm a detective. It's what I do. How much did the guns sell for?" Why was I asking about guns I had forgotten about?

"Five hundred cash for the pair."

"Fair market price?"

"About twenty-five percent below value."

"Which means?"

"Someone was in a hurry. They took less for cash. If you are willing to wait, you can usually get book value. Anyway, I may have more information for you within the next couple days. I still have a few leads out."

"Call them in," I said. "I already have more information than I need." And I did not want word getting back to Mundo Cruz that the guns were still being asked about. He might want a refund and Carmen might want a pound of flesh.

After I hung up with Sam I called Milton Brantferger.

"Milton, this is Harry Rice. Guess who I met today."

"Who?" He sounded bored.

"Your client. In fact, I just came from there."

"Really." He sounded unimpressed.

"Yeah. He even sent a driver for me. You better write this down. A guy in a red shirt and a black Hudson drove me to Galt Ocean Mile. You got that, Milton?"

"Red shirt. Black Hudson. Galt Ocean Mile."

"Now tear that up. I don't want to see you get hurt, Milton."

"What gives here, Harry? I paid you."

"You don't know who you're working for, do you?"

"Probably not," he admitted. "I think she's an intermediary."

"Black curly hair, green eyes, red Corvette, and sex oozing from her pores?"

"Good guess." He sounded impressed.

"Her name is Carmen. She works for Mundo Cruz," I said as if that said it all. And it should have.

I waited for a reaction.

Milton said, "Am I supposed to know him?"

"Milton, how old are you?" Maybe I should have been questioning my age. "Never mind," I said. "Just listen to me. You don't want to mess around on this guy's watch." I told Milton about the blue shirt, the white Cadillac, and the Bal Harbour high-rise. "I'm back at the Sand Bar now. I'll be here the rest of the evening. You better start following me again until you're instructed not to. I'm not going anywhere. After I close up here, I'm going home. Tomorrow morning I'm coming back and spending the whole day here."

"Wait a minute." He was annoyed. "I don't have time to—"

"You don't understand, Milton. You better make time. Mundo Cruz is the type to have you followed to make sure he's getting his nickel's worth. Trust me on this one, Milton. You've paid good money for this advice."

"Damn it, Harry. If I have to start following you again I'll want a refund."

"Yeah, and I'd like to spend the night with Laura Antonelli."

"What's that supposed to mean?"

"It means we all want something, Milton, but we don't always get it."

"Life is a series of disappointments." It was said with mockery, but it was right on the money.

"Very good, Milton. You get an A."

• • •

The jukebox was playing a blues tune about hard-hearted women and soft-headed men. Who was I to argue?

It was standing room only. The tables were filled and the bar was lined with men promising anything and women feigning interest in anticipation of better offers. I threaded my way through the crowd.

Carla was leaning across the bar, telling a slimy creature with teeth the size and color of popcorn kernels that he had been served his last drink and it was time for him to leave. The macho thing would have been for Nick or me to intervene, which is exactly why we let Carla handle it. A drunk being eighty-sixed by a woman will whine, but he'll comply. That same hundred-fifty-pound drunk will challenge a three-hundred-pound bouncer to a fight to the death. As expected, Carla prevailed and the drunk left.

I went over to her and started massaging her shoulders.

"Good job," I said. "You ready to call it a day?"

"Am I ever. As it is, I'm going to be late for my Verbally Battered Barmaids Support Group."

I laughed. "Where do you find all these women's groups?"

"Find them nothing. I start them."

"Get out of here." I swatted her playfully on the butt. Which was all right. We're that kind of friends. Nothing sexual. Just comfortable with one another. "I'll see you in the morning."

"You opening up?"

"Yeah. Take your time."

"Thanks. I'll try not to mention you by name at the meeting tonight. No promises though."

By seven-thirty that evening business had slowed enough that I had time to fiddle with the safe behind the bar. It usually takes me three tries to get the combination right. I put the money from Mundo Cruz in the safe and locked it.

At half past midnight Nick and I were the only two left in the bar. Nick locked up. Overall, it had been a profitable Friday for the Sand Bar. A good mixture of regulars and first time patrons, some local and some not. A traveling bachelor party of about a dozen stopped in. They quaffed a couple rounds before moving on to the next stop.

After Nick had locked the front door and turned down the lights, he said, "You going to tell me about the money you put in the safe?"

"Grab a seat," I said.

I filled a pitcher with beer and pulled two chilled mugs from the cooler. Nick was sitting at a table. I sat across from him and poured beer into the glasses. We each took one.

"To a good night's work," I said.

We took long swallows. Nothing like a well-earned cold beer.

"Start with the guy in the blue shirt you left here with this afternoon," Nick said between swallows.

"He works for Mundo Cruz."

Nick stared at me half in disbelief, like he hadn't heard right. "The same Mundo Cruz?"

I nodded. "The same."

"I thought he was dead. His money in the safe?"

I nodded and refilled our glasses. "Five thousand dollars."

"What's he get for five thousand dollars?"

"That's the funny thing. He doesn't get anything."

Nick took another swig of beer. "Does he know that?"

"Not really. He told me to forget about the Loftus gun collection."

"And he paid you five thousand dollars for that?"

"Yeah, he did. The thing is, I was ready to forget about the guns. There seems to be some question whether they were ever stolen. Yesterday Sam Maturano gave me a lead on one of the guns. It was at a pawnshop in Medley. I went there this morning. The pawnbroker tells me he bought the gun a few months before it was reported stolen. He has a ledger supporting his claim. What's more, the guy he bought it from fits Wade Loftus's description. So already I'm thinking something isn't right."

"You're quick that way."

"Experience," I said modestly. "Then this afternoon Sam tells me that he has found two more guns from the collection. A collector in Boca Raton has them. And he bought them a couple weeks before the guns were supposed to have been stolen. So if the guns were never stolen, there's nothing to recover, and no reward or finder's fee to be collected."

"You didn't tell Cruz this?"

I spread my hands. "At the time, I only knew about the one gun for sure."

Nick took a swallow of beer. "Why would he not want you looking for the guns, anyway? What's it to him?"

"He didn't share that information with me. You know

what's also curious about all this? Mundo Cruz's connection to Wade Loftus."

Nick said, "Maybe Cruz is a gun collector. Maybe Loftus sold Cruz some of the guns that were later reported stolen."

"So? What difference would it make to Cruz?"

Nick chewed on that a moment. "Maybe he's just doing a favor for his dealer. I don't know. What—you think Cruz stole the guns?"

"No," I said. "The thought had crossed my mind. But now I don't even know if any guns were stolen. Besides, even if the gun collection was intact, it would be nickel and dime stuff to someone like Cruz. Plus he says he's retired."

"What did Mrs. Loftus say when you told her that Mundo Cruz had made you an offer you didn't refuse."

"I haven't told her yet. I'll call her in the morning."

"You going to tell her that her husband was selling the guns before they were supposed to have been stolen?"

"I don't know what I'm going to tell her. Frankly, I'm not so sure that she didn't know what was going on. Think about it. How could she not notice that the collection was being depleted?"

Nick shrugged. "Perhaps the guns weren't kept on display. Maybe they were stored."

"Possibly," I conceded. "But suppose she did notice that the guns had been disappearing. Suppose that's why she hired me. Not to find the guns, but to prove they were not stolen, knowing all along that she wouldn't have to pay me anything because I couldn't recover guns that had previously been sold."

"Makes sense. She gets the information she wants for free," Nick said. "She that smart?"

"The question is, am I that dumb."

"You want me to field that one?"

"Wait a sec. Suppose Wade Loftus was replacing the guns he sold with cheap imitations. Then Eloise wouldn't know the guns were being sold off." Good old naive Harry Poppins, slow to believe ill of any woman.

Nick said, "What's his motive?"

"Money, what else? Maybe he needed money that he wanted to keep hidden from his wife. So he sells the guns—"

"And stages the burglary to cover up that he had been selling them."

"That way he collects twice," I said, picking up the theme. "First he sells the guns. Then he collects a second time from the insurance company. Of course he'd collect twice even if he didn't plan the theft. Maybe it was just lucky for him everything was stolen. It covered it up for him. Either way, though, he doesn't want me poking around. That's why he was upset when his wife told him she was hiring me. He doesn't want the insurance company to find out he collected on guns he no longer owned. I'm sure even the Florida bar must frown on lawyers committing insurance fraud."

"Only if they get caught." Mr. Cynic. Nick sipped his beer. "That still doesn't explain how Mundo Cruz is involved. Or who cut your lip, for that matter."

"The knife lady works for Cruz."

"Mundo Cruz an equal opportunity employer. Who'd a thunk it."

"I'll tell you, Nick, the more I think about this, the more I'm convinced that Wade Loftus brought Cruz in. Cruz mentioned Mrs. Loftus by name. Even with that, I'm still having trouble comprehending Cruz's relationship with Wade Loftus. Why would Cruz go through all this trouble and cash for Loftus? Something is missing."

"Son of a bitch," Nick mumbled.

"What?"

Nick's face twitched. "Loftus lied to us. He said he didn't know who cut you."

"It would appear he did. Put yourself in his place. Who you going to be more afraid of? Ozzie and Harriet or Mundo Cruz?"

"Yeah."

We finished off the beer.

"Let's go home," I said.

"So what are you going to tell Mrs. Loftus?"

"I don't know. I'll tell her I quit. Other than that, I'm not sure. I'm not even sure how much she already knows."

"You mean like was she taking advantage of you, playing you for the fool?"

"Shit. Woman ain't been born that can do that."

"Shit. Woman ain't been born that *can't* do that."

When Nick's right, he's right.

I went home and tried to sleep. I kept thinking about guns and Eloise and lawyers and Carmen and hoods. And then I started thinking about Mali. How much she meant to me. How much I wanted to talk to her. To see her. I was still thinking about Mali when someone started pounding on my front door at six-thirty Saturday morning.

sixteen

· · · · · · · · · ·

I slid out of bed without hurting myself. I eased on a pair of tattered denim cutoffs. I didn't look for a shirt. At six-thirty in the A.M., when someone is banging on my door, I'm not overly concerned with dressing spiffily or with making a fashion statement, as I once might have been in another lifetime.

I looked out the window. The morning sky was a sad and seedy gray, two shades brighter than my cheerless mood.

I went to the door and opened it.

Eloise Loftus stood there, fidgeting with a paper sack. She wore a not completely buttoned virginal white jump-suit. She was braless. Even in a sleepy daze some things are easier to distinguish than others.

She said, "I brought breakfast."

My speech circuits hadn't connected yet, so I just stepped aside and smelled the fresh coffee as she walked past. She went to the kitchen. I went to the bathroom.

Among other ablutions, I rinsed my mouth with warm water. The lip was less tender than yesterday and it was no longer impersonating Gibraltar. The swelling had finally begun to subside.

The kitchen table was set with coffee, orange juice, toasted English muffins, and assorted jelly samples. She was sitting with her back to the door. I sat next to her. The coffee was hot. Eloise was not.

She acknowledged my presence with a cold expression and said, "You didn't call me yesterday."

I blinked.

She said, "You told me you would call."

The whine in her voice made me flinch.

"It's too early for this," I muttered groggily.

"I waited for you to call." She was beginning to sound like a petulant child.

I gave her a hard stare. "That better not be why you're here."

It came out sounding more caustic than I had intended. I was having trouble mastering the subtleties of machismo etiquette. Which, in this case, worked to my advantage. Eloise was taken aback by my tone. No doubt unaccustomed to being talked to that way, she glared at me. Slowly the reproachful look in her eyes faded. She searched for a more suitable role with which to seize her reluctant audience. Her demeanor became one of worry. She was now a damsel in distress.

"Wade knows about us," she said with high drama. She lifted her eyes so I could see tears welling. She was good.

Tears work. Even contrived tears. I was teetering between compassion and impatience. Her insinuation about "us" annoyed me.

"What about 'us,' Eloise? What's there to know?" I sounded like Don Knotts cast in the part of the prosecuting attorney. I still hadn't decided between concern or anger.

Her eyes narrowed. That was not the response she had anticipated. I wasn't playing Galahad to her maiden. It looked like Deputy Barney Fife was about to be eaten alive by a rabid Elizabeth Taylor.

Eloise pointed an accusatory finger at me. "Don't play innocent with me, mister. Ever since you first saw me, you've been ogling me." It didn't help my defense any that I was peering reverently at her cleavage as she said that. If you want smart, see me after lunch. In the morning I'm usually at the Lost and Found window looking for my mind. "You've wanted me since we first met. You've been dropping double entendres after every comma—"

"That I haven't done."

"—and then when I show similar interest in you, you wait until after you've copped a feel and had an eyeful before becoming self-righteous."

"The point is, we stopped. Nothing happened."

Eloise was glowering. "Nothing happened? You want to tell Wade that fondling his wife's breasts is nothing?"

I spread a knifeful of jelly across an English muffin and then pushed the plate away. I never eat breakfast on an empty stomach.

"What makes you think Wade knows?" I asked resignedly.

"I told him." She was as pious as Opie telling Andy he had shot the bird.

I nodded. "Code of the condo couples?"

Her nostrils flared.

I said, "Did you tell him I got you pregnant?"

Her mouth tightened.

"Tell me, when Wade and I compare notes over cocktails," I said, "what should I say to him? Do you spit or swallow?"

I caught her hand in midair before she slapped me

silly. We were riveted eye to eye. Her arm relaxed. I released my grip.

She looked at me disgustedly, as though I had just told her that I had eloped with a camel.

"If you would just listen for a minute, I'll explain what happened." Her voice strained for control, but her eyes were seething.

Against my better judgment, I opened my mouth. "Explain it to the village priest," I said. "I'm not a welfare worker for the love-starved."

"How dare you judge me!" she snapped. "I don't see any woman sharing your life."

Ouch. She was better at this than I was. I almost countered with, "Yeah, but you ought to see the women that have left me." I didn't. Mainly because I wasn't really sure if they had left me or if I had left them.

I sipped some coffee instead.

"I intended to call you yesterday," I said quietly. "When I got back to the Sand Bar, business was heavy. I had to help out behind the bar. By the time it quieted down it was too late to call you. I was going to call this morning."

Her tense body began to relax like an inflatable doll with a slow leak.

"You found out something?" Her tone and manner were strictly business. It was as if we had just met. Perhaps we had.

I said, "I had the guns appraised against your inventory. My expert used several buyer's guides. Without seeing the guns, it seems the insurance company made an equitable settlement. Based on that, it no longer appears to be a profitable venture for me to pursue."

"What are you saying?"

"I'm saying I don't think it's in your best interest, or mine, for me to keep looking for the guns."

"You're giving up?" Her voice was dripping with contempt.

"No. I'm quitting."

"Because of one expert's opinion?"

"Yes."

"What about the lead you said you had on one of the guns?"

"Let it go, Eloise."

She shook her head. "I'll hire someone else."

"You'd be throwing money away."

"Money? Is that what this is about? You want to make sure you get paid? What was it? Five thousand dollars for two weeks? I'll pay it."

"I don't want your money."

"Why?" she persisted. "Tell me why."

I sat back and picked up a glass of orange juice. It was lukewarm. I leaned forward, resting my elbows on the table. "Remember the other day when you told me that Wade had told you everything?"

She nodded.

"Well," I continued, "I don't think he did."

Eloise kept looking at me. She didn't say anything.

"I've located three of the guns," I said. "One in a pawnshop in Medley. A private collector in Boca has the other two. The guns were bought before your apartment was burglarized. I think Wade was selling the guns."

She took it all in. "I don't believe it," she said unconvincingly.

"What don't you believe?"

"I don't believe any of it."

"I'm sure about the guns."

"But not Wade?"

"Nothing I can prove. Wade fits the description of the man who sold the gun to the pawnshop."

"What about the collector in Boca? Who did he buy the guns from?"

"I didn't ask."

She thought about that. "I need to know for sure about Wade. I want you to find out for me, Harry."

She reached across the table and placed her hand on mine. She was leaning forward. The jumpsuit fell open enough to show her breast if you looked from just the right angle. With a minor adjustment, I was sitting at just the right angle. It was so tempting. I pulled my hand away. Harry Presley can recognize a devil in disguise three out of ten times.

"I quit," I said.

She stared at me disdainfully. She could change expression as easily as a child loses interest in a toy. "I won't let you quit. I'll file a complaint with whoever I have to, whoever regulates your license."

"I guess a letter of recommendation is out of the question."

"You're a smart-ass son of a bitch."

"I've been called worse."

"I haven't even started on you."

I smiled. "After what I've been through since meeting you, a few names ain't going to bother me. I've been cut, stitched, followed, and kidnapped. Badmouth me and sneer if it will make you feel better. I'll try to stay awake for your performance."

She looked confused. I wished my cable company offered as many channels as Eloise had moods.

I said, "Think about it. Why would someone cut me and tell me to forget about the guns? Because the guns weren't stolen. Who had something to hide? Wade did. If it came out that he had sold the guns that you reported stolen, Wade could be brought up on insurance fraud. He had to scare me off. Doesn't that tell you anything?"

She admitted nothing. At least to me. "You said kidnapped?"

I nodded. "Ever hear of Mundo Cruz?"

That surprised her. She recovered quickly, but I had already seen the reaction. The name registered. It meant something to her. Maybe a blast from the past, an old family friend, a name from a newsreel. Or maybe she couldn't connect Mundo Cruz with her husband. Neither could I.

She said, "Wasn't he some kind of . . ."

"Yes, he was some kind. Cruz told me to forget about the guns." I didn't tell her about his cash incentive program. "Still think Wade told you everything?"

"That's why you're quitting, isn't it? You're afraid."

"That's one way of putting it."

"What about me? What do I do now?"

"Nothing. You're not out any money. The insurance company paid you what the guns were worth."

"Forget the guns! I'm talking about Wade."

"Tell him what you know. Tell him what I told you. That will put you one up on him in the score column."

"What's that suppose to mean?"

"That's what this is all about, isn't it? You told Wade about me massaging your mammaries to get back at him for Lola."

"You're a crude bastard."

"That hurts coming from one so delicate. Go home, Eloise. Tell Wade you know he was selling the guns. That will give you the win in this round of your marital war games."

So it went for another five minutes. We continued to attack each other's psyche on a very mature level. We didn't stick our tongues out at one another or do anything childish.

As she walked out the door I called after her, "Thanks for the wake-up call."

I closed the door on Eloise Loftus. On Wade Loftus. Time to get back to the business of running a bar. No more guns. No more Mundo Cruz. No more Carmen. No more sharks reading legal books. No more teacher's dirty looks. I was forever through with Wade and Eloise. Or so I thought.

Four days later I was arrested for the murder of Wade Loftus.

seventeen

·············

This is what the police had: I was picked up driving the victim's Volvo. The victim's Rolex watch was in the Sand Bar safe. There was a witness who saw the victim's wife leave my house arm in arm with me, saw us kiss before getting into her car and driving off together. A witness who saw the victim's wife leaving my house early one morning. The victim's wife admitted she had been physically intimate with me. My fingerprints were in the victim's office. The last phone number dialed from that office was to my home number. I was the last person to see the victim alive. The victim's body was found in the trunk of my car. And two days before the body was found, in front of witnesses, I threatened to kill him.

• • •

Detective Stokesberry held a burning match over the bowl of his pipe, drawing short breaths until he was sure the tobacco was lit. He was a large man, which unfortunately is the only qualification required by too many police departments. I put him in his mid-thirties, though he dressed more like Joe Friday than like Sonny Crockett. His eyes were intense, but his voice suggested ennui.

Stokesberry withdrew the pipe from his mouth. "All things considered," he said, "what would you think?"

"I'd think I was a victim of circumstances."

"I wouldn't. Let's go over it again."

"Give it a rest already, Stokesberry. Everything is circumstantial."

He shrugged. "I work with what I have."

"And you don't have a motive. Why would I kill Wade Loftus?"

"For the same reason you threatened to kill him."

"I've already explained that."

"So you killed him for money. Revenge. Lust. Maybe it was manslaughter. Maybe Wade Loftus attacked you in a jealous rage when he discovered you were having an affair with his wife. Perhaps defending yourself—"

"I accidentally stabbed him a half-dozen times?"

Stokesberry smiled for the first time in over an hour. "It doesn't work for me, either. No matter. Motive is not the problem. Nor is opportunity. You were the last person to see him alive."

"Let's not forget his killer."

"That's not you?"

"I didn't do it."

"Your fingerprints were in his office."

"Imagine that."

"How did they get there?"

"I sell them at the Sand Bar. Ten fingerprints for a dollar."

"Cute. How many times were you in his office."

"Twice."

"Count them for me."

"The first time was the day after his wife hired me."

"To do what?"

"Ask her. The next time was a couple days later."

Stokesberry looked at his notes. "That would be the time you showed up with your—and I quote—'hired thug to put Wade Loftus through a psychological chamber of horrors.' "

I cringed. I had forgotten I had said that the day Nick turned Wade Loftus upside down in his chair. I admitted saying it.

Stokesberry laced his fingers behind his head and tilted back in his chair. With the pipe in his mouth, he was doing his best to look like a pensive Sherlock Holmes.

"When was the last time you saw Wade Loftus?" he said.

"I've told you three times already."

"Tell me again."

"Fine. I never met the man in my life."

Stokesberry took the pipe out of his mouth. "I'm getting paid for being here. You want this to last all week? Fine with me."

"Sunday morning."

Stokesberry sat upright. "Sunday morning," he said aloud as he wrote it down, even though the interview was being tape recorded. "That would be the day after you told him you were going to kill him?"

"Yes."

"Where did you meet him?"

"He came to the Sand Bar."

Stokesberry rubbed his chin. "Let's see. Saturday he comes to your bar, physically assaults you and your barmaid, and you threaten to kill him. The next day he returns to the bar, gives you his ten-thousand-dollar watch and his fifty-thousand-dollar car." He closed his eyes and meditated for a moment. He looked at me. "Why do I have a problem with that?"

"He didn't give me the watch. He put it up as collateral."

"Collateral for what?"

"I told you. It was against my retainer. It was Sunday morning, the banks were closed, and I wouldn't accept a check from him. I told him I wanted cash."

"Why?"

"I was trying to put him off for another day. I didn't feel like driving to Jacksonville. I wanted to wait until Monday. He was insistent that I start right away. He offered to put up his watch to guarantee my fee."

"He was hiring you."

"Of course he was hiring me."

"Because you threatened to kill him, he hired you. Duh, I'm just a big dumb cop, maybe you can explain that to me."

I looked at him. "At least we agree on something."

He flushed, but I think he realized he had set himself up. He let it pass. "What was he hiring you for?"

"To find a missing person."

"Who?"

"A go-go girl."

"Lola."

"Very good, Detective."

"We'll get back to her. Why did he give you his car?"

"He didn't give it to me. It was a loaner. Loftus believed that Lola was in Jacksonville, staying with friends. He wanted me to go find her. My car wouldn't make it out of Broward County. He wouldn't authorize the cost of a rental car. He suggested I take his car."

"Why did he want you to find Lola?"

"Ask him."

Stokesberry arched an eyebrow. "Did you find her?"

"No."

"What were you supposed to do if you found her?"

"Call him. Tell him where she was. Who she was with."

Stokesberry shifted gears. "How long have you known the victim's wife?"

"Too long."

"Oh?"

"It's not what you think."

"What do I think?"

"I just meant I have had nothing but trouble since I met her."

"When was that?"

"I don't know. Maybe a week and a half ago."

"How'd you meet her?"

"She came to the Sand Bar to hire me."

"As a bartender?"

"Private investigator."

"Your license still good?"

"It was when I came in here."

"What'd she hire you for?"

"Ask her."

"I will. Did you have sex with her?"

"Ask her."

"I did. I'm asking you now."

"Define sex."

"Tell me what happened and I'll tell you if that's sex."

"I caressed her breasts."

"Outside or inside the blouse?"

"Her breasts were exposed."

"How'd they get that way?"

"You enjoying this?"

"It's what I live for. It's what makes being a homicide detective worthwhile. Answer the question."

"I freed them during heavy petting."

"So you kissed her, too?"

"Yes."

"What else?"

"That's all."

"Nothing more?"

"That's all."

"That took all night?"

"She wasn't there all night."

"A neighbor says she saw Mrs. Loftus sneaking out of your house early Saturday morning. Just hours before you threatened to kill Mr. Loftus."

"What time did the neighbor say Mrs. Loftus snuck into my house?"

"The neighbor didn't say."

"How convenient. Let's not clutter your case with facts."

"How many times did you entertain Mrs. Loftus?"

"Just that once."

He sucked on his pipe while he tapped a pencil on the table.

"Well?" I said.

"Well what?"

"Is that sex?"

He pulled the pipe out of his mouth and stared hard into my eyes. "It is if you're doing that with my wife." He flipped through his notes. "What time did Wade Loftus come to the Sand Bar on Sunday?"

"In the morning. Before opening. Maybe eleven."

"He called your home first?"

"No. My home number is unlisted. He just showed up."

"How'd his body end up in your car?"

"I'd say the killer put it there."

"How did the killer know it was your car?"

"I don't know that the killer did know it was my car. Maybe it was just because the car was there. Loftus had taken my car, since I had his."

"Or maybe the killer did know it was your car, and he's just trying to frame you."

"I like that."

"Or maybe you thought by putting the body in your car the police would think you were too smart to leave such an easy trail."

"I like the other idea better."

"I thought you might."

The door to the interrogation room opened. In walked Detective-Lieutenant Stranahan. He looked around the room as if it were the first time he had seen it. He looked at me as if he hoped it would be the last time he would see me. He was the same size as Stokesberry. He may have been fifty, but he wouldn't have been carded seeking a senior citizen's discount. He hadn't aged well. He was wearing a charcoal gray suit over a white shirt and a gray tie. He turned a chair around and straddled it like Hoppy mounting Topper.

"All right," Stranahan grunted. "Now you've had your tune-up. Run your story past me. Don't miss a thing."

"Where do you want me to start?" I said. "When his wife hired me?"

"No. I heard that part." He nodded toward the two-way mirror. "Start with Saturday afternoon at the Sand Bar when you threatened to kill the dead man."

eighteen

• • • • • • • • • • •

The heat was unforgiving. Not even the hint of a breeze. The ocean and the palm trees were as still as oil on canvas. The clammy air was so thick, it was like looking at a Monet through a sheet of gauze. The only motion on the beach was a family of sunburned tourists lumbering by on the Broadwalk.

It was Saturday afternoon. Lunch was ordered by the bottle by a few dehydrated sun worshipers who sat at the bar guzzling cold beer. The ceiling fans were set on high speed, providing nominal relief from the stifling temperature.

I was up to my elbows in the sink, washing glasses. Carla was talking to a gray-bearded customer about New Orleans. The customer looked like Hemingway just in from landing a marlin. I was sure the effect was not accidental.

A couple that could have been Mr. and Ms. Universe contestants walked in. They sat at a table. I told Carla I would take their order. I dried my hands, sucked in my gut, and walked over to the table.

They ordered a carafe of white wine.

I was hit from behind. I didn't see or hear it coming. Carla shouted, but whatever she said was drowned out by the ringing sensation in my head.

I took a wobbly step forward before a long arm hooked around my neck, snapping my head back and shutting off my air supply. For added leverage, a knee was plowed into the middle of my back, while the pressure across my throat was increased. I stomped on a foot planted on the floor next to mine. Whoever it was lost his balance and stumbled. We fell over sideways. The fall broke the hold on my neck. Unfortunately, my head hit the side of a table before landing with a thud on the floor. The blows to my head, coupled with the state of dismay my mind was in from the sudden and unexpected attack, left me stunned.

Wade Loftus sprang to his feet as if he was propelled by some demonic force. He aimed a kick and launched it into my kidneys. The blow registered a ten on the Rice scale of pain. For an encore, Loftus followed with a kick to the base of my skull.

My lights were dimming.

While the bar patrons watched the floor show, Carla raced from behind the bar to my defense. She grabbed Loftus by his hair and yanked. Loftus yelped. He swung around and slapped Carla with the full force of a backhand. Only then did Mr. Universe intervene.

• • •

"Did you call the police?"

I could see that Stranahan was serious. Maybe he had to ask the question because the tape was running and someday one of his superiors would listen to the recording right before annual performance-appraisal time.

I said no.

Stranahan said, "Why not?"

"I could tell you it never occurred to me, or I could get philosophical with you. You have a preference?"

He shrugged. "It's your story."

"To be honest with you, I never thought about calling the police."

"I like it when you're honest with me."

"Then you're going to love me."

"What happened next?"

• • •

Someone put money in the jukebox.

Mr. Universe's massive arms grabbed Loftus in a full-nelson check. The barside spectators nipped at their drinks and stared at me sprawled on the floor. As my sense returned, I managed to push myself up to a kneeling position. I thought about ramming Wade Loftus with a head-butt to his rib cage, but I couldn't see any sense in it. I hit him. Then he hits me back. What would be gained? There's nothing glorious about a barroom brawl. Especially when your opponent has a six-inch reach advantage.

The jukebox played on.

I stood up, careful not to do any more damage to myself. Bells were still echoing in my skull. Carla slid her shoulder under my arm so I could lean on her while my legs steadied. That's when I noticed that the side of her face was puffy where Loftus had struck her. My eyes fixed sharply on Loftus, who was still dangling, wild-eyed and sweating, from Mr. Universe's grasp.

The muscles in my neck tightened as I took a step toward him. I flexed my fingers, which were aching to rip him apart—not for what he did to me, but for hitting Carla. That act ignited a hate in me I didn't know existed.

My thoughts must have been deadly and piercing. Wade Loftus was having no trouble reading me correctly.

Tight-jawed, and in the low voice of an exorcist's nightmare, I said, "Get out of here. If I ever see you again, you're as good as dead."

And I meant it.

The jukebox seconded that emotion.

• • •

Stranahan loosened his tie and studied me quietly. Stokesberry was leaning back in his chair, puffing on his pipe. After a brief silence Stokesberry began the questioning.

"So you did threaten to kill him."

"In so many words, yes."

"Did you mean it?"

"It was said in the heat of the moment. It was hot. He hit me. He hit Carla. I was angry. I meant it."

"Do you always threaten to kill people when you're angry?"

"No."

"How often?"

"Never."

"So you must have been serious."

"Yes, I was serious."

"After you threatened him, what did he say?"

"Nothing. He left."

"Did he say why he attacked you?"

"No. I thought it was because of his wife. Because he was jealous."

"That wasn't it?"

"No."

"If he didn't tell you, how do you know?"

"He told me later."

"When."

"Sunday."

Stokesberry nodded. "Let's stay with Saturday for a moment. The whole time he was in the Sand Bar he never said a word. He assaults you and your barmaid—"

"Her name is Carla."

"Carla Meadows?"

"Yes."

"He attacks you and Carla Meadows and doesn't say a word. Doesn't that seem strange to you?"

"Of course it seemed strange."

"No shit," mumbled Stranahan.

Stokesberry glanced nervously at the older detective, then at me. "What happened after Loftus left the Sand Bar?" Stokesberry said.

"I bought a carafe of white wine for Mr. Universe and his girlfriend."

"Why?"

"Because he had helped out."

"Christ, Stokesberry," Stranahan said. "We'll be here all night at this rate." Stranahan turned to me. "Anything else happen on Saturday that is pertinent to this case, Rice? And don't bullshit me."

"No."

"You didn't see or talk to Mrs. Loftus after her husband left?"

"No."

"How long did you stay at the Sand Bar afterwards?"

"I was there until about ten P.M."

"Is that when you closed?"

"No. I went home then. Nick Triandos, the night bartender, was still there. He locks up at closing."

"You went straight home?"

"Yes."

"Did you call anyone."

"No. I licked my wounds and went to bed."

"All right. When was the next time you saw or spoke to either Mr. or Mrs. Loftus?"

"That would be Sunday morning."

"Tell us about Sunday morning."

nineteen

. . . .

On Sundays the Sand Bar opens at noon. I had a ten-thirty appointment to meet a vendor at the bar, so I went to the beach early to get in some exercise. I alternated between swimming and walking on the packed sand along the shore. The beach was relatively quiet. The only people I saw before nine o'clock were a teenaged couple, fast-walking like they were late for Sunday school.

The morning was heating up faster than a rookie relief pitcher. It had the makings of another scorcher.

After swimming about a mile, I walked five miles, and then showered off the sticky film of dried saltwater caked on my skin.

At ten-thirty I was sitting in the Sand Bar with a cold glass of cranberry juice, listening to Stacey Shore plot her next career move.

Stacey was a woman of many interests. She was past forty, but her life savings consisted of her next paycheck. Over the years she had been a protest singer who had once opened for Richie Havens, a waitress in a Washington, D.C., health food restaurant, a poet, an artist's model, a Zen dance instructor, a Kwik Chek cashier, a Chinese clown, a school bus driver, a barber, a wife for hire, a night security guard, a washroom attendant in Belgium, and a hospital aide. She was now a Tom's sales representative.

Stacey's personal life was even less stable. There had been more boyfriends and lovers than she could name. She had been married four times. Her first marriage was to her high-school geometry teacher. She was seventeen. He was twenty years older. Eighteen months later she divorced him because he was too immature. Husband number two was a roadie. He left her to go to Janis Joplin's wake and never returned. The third marriage was to the man "who was circumcised twice." That's all she ever said about him and I never asked for details. Husband the fourth was a Colombian who paid Stacey twenty-five thousand dollars to marry him. He became a U.S. resident, and a year later Stacey was a four-time divorcee. She said she was living proof that there was life after love.

It didn't faze Stacey that others thought her professional and personal stats were those of a loser. She'd shrug it off and admit she had squandered her life enjoying it.

After I finished placing a monthly order for nuts and chips, Stacey began to tell me about her plans to open a used-book store on the Broadwalk.

"What made you decide on that?" I said.

"Vibes," she said.

"Vibes?" I knew better than to question female mysticism, but that didn't stop me. "What year did you wake up in this morning?"

Stacey wriggled her eyebrows. "Why, in the year that ought to be, of course." She giggled. "I'm going to write a book, Harry. Can you imagine a more conducive atmosphere for creating than being on the beach surrounded by the spirits of Queequeg and Kilgore Trout?"

"Can't say that I can."

"Guess what kind of book I'm going to write."

"Teamster erotica?"

Stacey laughed. "I love it, but no."

"A sci-fi autobiography?"

Stacey pretended to be offended. "Why, Harry, you're not suggesting I'm spacey, are you?"

"I only read the tea leaves, I don't interpret them."

"Well, you read them wrong, my friend. I'm writing a police procedural. Want to hear it?"

"You brought it with you?"

"I've memorized it. I just started it. It's only a paragraph."

"By all means, then. Let's hear it."

Stacey cleared her throat and bowed slightly, like a second-grader about to recite the story of how Bernie saved Christmas. "The Wrinkled Dream, by Stacey Shore. Chapter one. The eggs cackled like a wicked witch in the burning margarine. Woolly clouds of steam sputtered across the kitchen. The radio on the draining board was tuned to the local college FM station. The announcer, who sounded like his scrotum was caught in his throat, said, 'Today's operatic selection is from Heinz Herring's "Portrait of a Fish." ' The woman lying on the floor heard nothing. Nor did she feel the coarse tongue of the cat pull along her nose. 'Portrait of a Fish' was wasted on a cat who preferred the twang of a steel guitar. A uniformed police officer stood in the doorway, looking at the body on the floor. He pushed back his hat and thought, this is a case for Lieutenant Doster McGlamory, Macon Homicide."

Stacey smiled and bowed again. "Ta-da. That's all for now, folks. So?"

"So," I said, "Tom's loss will be literature's gain."

"Well, I'll tell you this. Writing a novel is a lot more fun than writing poems about the gargoyle of Notre Dame."

"There's nothing verse."

Stacey rolled her eyes. "I think I'll leave on that note. I have other stops to make. Your order will be here tomorrow. Call me if you need anything else. Otherwise I'll see you in a few weeks."

"Bring more chapters," I said.

She blew me a kiss and left.

Ten minutes later I was cleaning the sink in the ladies' room when I heard a tapping on the front window. I ignored it, hoping it would go away. The bar didn't open for another hour. The tapping persisted. I dried my hands and walked out to the bar to see who it was.

Standing framed in the window, with bright sunlight as a backdrop, Wade Loftus resembled an animated shadow begging in semaphore. It amazed me that he had the nerve to return after what had happened the day before. I stared at him in disbelief. Then I actually felt a twinge of pity for him. He looked so lonely and lost, like Kukla without Ollie. What the hell. I opened the door and let him in.

He wore a short-sleeved Jungle Jim shirt, complete with epaulets. He had on light-weight olive-colored slacks, and a matching scarf tied loosely around his neck. The courage to dress ridiculously. A Yuppie's merit badge. A pith helmet for Christmas.

"Back for a rematch?" I said.

He shook his head. "No. Can we sit down?"

We went into the office and sat.

I waited for him to speak.

He hemmed and hawed and finally said, "Are you going to file charges?"

I could have gloated; we both knew I had the upper

hand. I nodded sagely, like a benevolent dictator. "I imagine the Florida bar would frown on a member being charged with assault and battery. If you're here because you're afraid of losing your union card, forget it. I don't do things that way."

• • •

"No, you prefer to take the law into your own hands," Stokesberry said.

Stranahan and I looked at Stokesberry.

I said, "You want to tell it, Stokesberry?"

He said no.

Stranahan mumbled something about how you can learn more with your ears than your mouth.

I continued.

• • •

Loftus said, "That's not why I'm here." He sounded weary. He looked up at me. "I want to talk to you. I tried to call you at home this morning, but your number wasn't in the directory. I thought if I came by here you might be in." He nodded to himself, as if he was debating something. "I think I want to hire you."

We stared at each other. It was quiet enough to hear a fly fart. Life-encounters with the Loftuses. Did it ever end?

I said, "Go away. I'm not for hire."

"At least let me talk to you," he snapped. Just as quickly, his tone changed. "Please, just listen to me." Like wife, like husband.

I said, "How much money do you have with you?"

"Now? On me?"

"Yes, now."

He pulled out his wallet and leafed through the bills tucked inside. He hesitated for a moment, like a poker player contemplating a bluff.

He said, "A hundred and forty dollars."

"Give it to me."

"What for?"

"Ten minutes."

He looked questioningly at me. "I don't understand."

"You want to talk to me, you're going to have to pay for my time. That's how I do things."

"Instead of filing a complaint?"

"Among other things."

"That's tantamount to extortion."

"Go home, Wade."

"Wait a minute. That's a lot of money for ten minutes. That's more than I charge."

"I should hope so. It's only forty dollars for ten minutes. The hundred goes in Carla's tip jar."

"Carla?"

"The lady you hit yesterday. The lady you assaulted. Consider it a fine."

He considered it. He handed me the money.

"It wasn't insurance fraud," he said.

"But you were selling the guns?"

"You mean from the collection?"

"Of course from the collection. What else?"

"Yes," he said. "I was selling off the collection."

"Without your wife knowing about it?" I don't know why that was important to me. Maybe I wanted to believe I hadn't been set up completely.

He shook his head. "I didn't want her to know."

"How did you keep it from her?"

"It was easy. The guns were kept stored in drawers and boxes in the closet. Eloise had no interest in the guns, other than what they were worth. She wouldn't know the difference between a derringer and a twelve-gauge shotgun."

"How many had you sold?"

"Half a dozen."

"Why were you selling them?"

He bristled. "It wasn't for insurance fraud."

There was something he didn't want to tell me.

"So you said. That's not what I asked."

Loftus sat there trying to devise an answer, while I tried to figure out what it was he wasn't saying.

I took a shot. "You were getting ready to break off the marriage, weren't you."

He looked at me and nodded.

I laughed to myself. "So when you attacked me yesterday, you weren't defending your wife's virtue."

Loftus remained quiet.

I said, "I blew your plan to squirrel away as much as you could from your joint holdings before you went for the divorce."

He nodded. "For a bartender, you're not a bad detective." He said it almost grudgingly. "That's one of the reasons I want to hire you." It seemed that all the Loftuses needed multiple reasons to hire me. "The other reason is, you already know the background. The fewer people who know, the better."

"Before you go any further with this, let's not forget that your buddy, Señor Cruz, has already asked me as a personal favor to forget about your gun collection."

Loftus's face clouded. He canted his head. "My buddy? What are you talking about?"

"Mundo Cruz."

Loftus looked sincerely confused. "Mundo Cruz?"

"Yeah. Are you telling me you don't know Mundo Cruz?"

"Well, I've heard of him, but I certainly don't know

him. What does Mundo Cruz have to do with my gun collection?"

Now I was confused. I could almost feel my mind go limp. Just when I thought I knew what was going on, it was begin at the beginning all over again.

I shook my head. "I have no idea."

"Well, it doesn't matter." Loftus sounded as if he was trying to convince a jury. "What I want to hire you for has nothing to do with the gun collection."

I closed my eyes and took a deep breath. I don't know why I continued to listen to him.

I heard him say, "I want you to find Elsbeth for me."

I thought about that. He wanted me to find Elsbeth. How nice. Who was Elsbeth? I hoped it was his dog. Being a trained professional, I knew what I had to do. I opened my eyes and asked him, "Who's Elsbeth?"

"Lola," he said simply.

"Lola," I repeated. "Lola, the naked-dancer-with-the-blue-owl-tattoo Lola?"

"Yes."

"The Lola who stole the gun collection that this has nothing to do with?"

He shook his head. "No. No, she didn't have a choice. They forced her to do that. She explained all that to me. I think she's in Jacksonville." He pulled a slip of paper from his shirt pocket. "Or she could be in Saint Augustine. I have some addresses of her friends up there. You can check these first. She said she had some family there, too. She told me to let her know when I had made up my mind."

As he was rambling on, it hit me. He knew who Lola was. He had been lying about her.

"Not completely," he said when I confronted him with my newfound truth. "It's true I didn't meet her at the nightclub for the first time. She came to my office. She had seen my ad in the yellow pages for sports and entertainment law. She wanted to hire me. As a sort of agent. I told her I would think about it and come see her show one night."

"Ah," I said. "So it was a business call. You were going to the aid of a helpless naked girl. What a guy."

Loftus ignored me. "When Eloise went out of town I went to Fort Bush looking for Lola. The rest of what I told you is what happened."

"For the most part," I said. "You've left out quite a lot."

He acknowledged that with a nod.

"And now you want me to find her for you?" I said.

"Yes."

"If not for the guns, then why?"

Wade Loftus made a choking sound as he said, "I love her. I want her to know that I'm ready to marry her."

twenty

· · · · · · · · ·

Stranahan and Stokesberry regarded me skeptically, as if I was holding something back, which of course I was. I did not tell them about Mundo Cruz & Co. Unless, and until, I was sure that Cruz's parlor tricks had killed Wade Loftus, I was not about to implicate him in a murder. There's a direct correlation between a private investigator's life expectancy and his ability to know when to implicate and when not to implicate.

Stranahan leaned back in his chair. His eyes never left me. I felt self-conscious, as if I was being accused of drinking the chocolate milk simply because I had a chocolate milk mustache.

Stokesberry started leafing through his notes, obviously uneasy with the silence and uncomfortable at the prospect of breaking it.

If Stranahan was trying to manipulate us with the silence, he was doing an excellent job. After six hours of sitting in that hard chair, I was ready to confess to the Lindbergh kidnapping in return for a last meal of *pasta aglio e oglio*. Even Stokesberry looked ready to confess to killing Wade Loftus.

"Not a bad storyteller," Stranahan said finally, almost admiringly. "You're a real smooth-talker."

"My friends call me Cyrano Rice," I said.

Stranahan nodded slowly, still looking at me. "Everything's a joke, huh? A man's dead, you want to make with the funny. You must think it's hysterical when a plane goes down."

There wasn't much I could say to that, so I did an uncharacteristically bright thing and did just that, said nothing.

Stranahan began drumming his fingers on the table. "Stay with me now. Wade Loftus wanted you to find Elsbeth, a.k.a. Lola, because he loved her and wanted to marry her. He gives you his watch as collateral against your fee." He mulled that over for a second. He said, "He loans you his car to drive to Jacksonville to find this Lola. Right?"

I nodded. "Right."

"You give him your car because your car won't make it to Jacksonville."

"That's a question?"

"That's a question."

"That's what happened. If you'd seen my car you'd—"

"I've seen your car."

Of course he had. My car was the crime scene where the body had been discovered.

Stranahan continued. "You exchanged cars. Then what? Did you leave for Jacksonville right away?"

"No," I said. "It was a few hours later. I worked the noon crowd at the bar with Carla. I left the Sand Bar about two-thirty. I went home, threw a few things into a gym bag. After that I drove to Saint Augustine. I got in around midnight and checked into a motel."

"Which one?" Stokesberry said, his pencil cocked and ready to scribble my response.

"The Spanish Quarter Inn. It's on Castillo Drive, or Avenue. Something like that."

"What was your room number?"

I shrugged and said nothing.

Stokesberry raised an eyebrow and smiled like a sadistic nun who has just discovered a six-year-old who hasn't done his catechism. "You don't remember your room number?"

"You got me. I'll plea-bargain to that charge."

"For crissakes, Stokesberry, what difference does it make?" said a very annoyed Detective Stranahan. He turned to me and said, "What else?"

I said, "Monday morning I drove to Jacksonville. I spent all day checking the addresses on the list Loftus gave me. There were addresses that the Jehovah's Witnesses couldn't have found. They were nonexistent street numbers, spread out all over the city. Which was a lot of territory to cover. The city limits and the county boundaries are the same. It was a wasted day. I didn't find one good address. It took most of the day to check them all. It was about seven P.M. by the time I got back to Saint Augustine."

"Where did you stay?" Stokesberry asked. I was beginning to suspect he was a slow learner.

"Same place, same room, whatever number it was. I never checked out."

Like a scarecrow without a brain, he had to ask, "Why didn't you stay in Jacksonville?"

Stranahan shot Stokesberry a go-to-your-room look. It was so quiet that death could have taken a lesson.

To ease Stokesberry's tension I said, "I like Saint Augustine better."

Stranahan was still glaring at Stokesberry when he asked me what I did on Tuesday.

"Same thing as Monday, except I did it in Saint Augustine."

"Same results? All bad addresses?"

"All but one. It was a vacant house with a For Rent sign out front."

• • •

It was a small, concrete block house with a gravel and tar roof. Big enough for two bedrooms and one bathroom, but it would have been a tight squeeze. The chalky, weather-beaten paint was peeling off in broken-heart-shaped flakes. There was only the memory of a pink that had stayed out in the Florida sun too long. The lawn was dirt and patches of brown grass. No trees. No dreams to give away. Fringe housing for mere mortals.

I got the rental agent's name from the sign and the address from a phone book at a 7-Eleven. Lesson three, Introduction to Private Investigation, Beach Heroes University.

The rental agent's office was in a strip shopping center wedged between a Chinese takeout and a discount women's wear emporium. There was also a drug store and a dollar movie theater featuring *Ernest Gets a Blow Job* or some such Ernest epic.

The office smelled of Sucrets marinating in port wine. One wall was papered with rental listings tacked into the plaster. The furniture was stuff that had more than likely been rescued from a Dumpster. A desk, a card table, a sunken couch, a magazine rack, a telephone, and a woman with red-framed glasses who undoubtedly idolized Sally Jessy and who may have understood the mysterious appeal of Michael Bolton. She was talking rental agent's talk into the phone.

"Security is always required. No. No interest. Read

your contract. No. Not now. I have a customer waiting. Yes. Bye. No. Bye. No."

She hung up, cocked her head, and smiled at me.

"Hiya," she said with a big, oft-practiced realtor's smile. "I'm DeDe Wysong. Whatever you need, I got it. I got houses. I got cottages. I got beachfront condos. I got efficiencies. I got expensive. I got cheap. I got everything in between. You want it, I got it."

"I'm sure you do, DeDe," I said. Her smile grew. "What I want is information." Her smile shrank faster than testicles in a bucket of ice water. I told her the address I was interested in.

She lit a cigarette. "What about it?"

"I want to know who lived there."

She nodded, glancing at her watch. "If the information is on me, then I guess lunch is on you."

"I guess it is. Chinese takeout?"

She sucked on her cigarette. "What's your name?"

"Harry."

"No such luck, Harry."

I said, "This lunch is going to cost me, isn't it?"

DeDe smiled again. "Yes, but not nearly as much as those people cost me."

It was one of those trendy restaurants where people drank fancy, bottled Canadian springwater naturally flavored with nature's own chemicals; where perfect women, untouched by human hands, waited for perfect men, who spent more on their hair than on their education, to spirit them away to that castle with the white picket fence.

The prices on the menu were no surprise. The food was. What the sugar industry is to the Everglades, what Mr. Ed is to thoroughbred horse racing, that's what this chef was to food preparation.

DeDe loved it.

"Had enough?" I said.

She genteelly swirled the ice in her cocktail glass, her third. She nodded contentedly. "Now, what was it you wanted to know?"

"How long has that house been vacant?"

"February," she said without hesitation.

"Who were the last tenants?"

"You don't know?"

"No."

She sat back and lit a cigarette. "Just what is it you're after?"

"I'm looking for a young woman."

"Elsbeth," she said ruefully.

"Do you know where she is?"

DeDe shook her head. "Haven't the foggiest. Haven't seen her since the funeral."

"Funeral?"

"Elsbeth's father. They lived in that house."

"How well did you know them?"

Her eyes narrowed. "How much do you know?"

"I don't know anything. I wasn't implying anything, either. I don't even know Elsbeth. I'm a private investigator. I've been hired to find her. That address is the only lead I have."

DeDe sipped her drink, then took a long drag of nicotine and tar. "Her father's name was Latham. He was a card-carrying drunk. That's what killed him, and that's what kept Elsbeth from having a life. Since she was fifteen she worked to support her father, his habit, and herself. And she was still able to finish high school. Where that poor girl found the energy to enroll in the junior college and still work full time is enough to make you believe in God. She never had any social life. She was pretty enough. She could have been a model if she knew how to take care of herself. She was just very shy and quiet.

You hardly knew she was there. Everything was for her father. It was like she was the parent. Latham wasn't a bad man. He wasn't abusive or anything like that. Actually he was a very gentle man. He just drank all the time and wallowed in self-pity. I guess Elsbeth felt sorry for him, too. Maybe that was what they had in common." She took another drag on her cigarette.

I don't know what I had expected to hear, but that wasn't it. I ran the information through my data bank. It didn't compute. How did the quiet, shy Elsbeth become the exhibitionist Lola? Were her only options that extreme? From wallflower to stripper? What caused the abrupt transition?

"Tell me more about Elsbeth," I said, redirecting DeDe's thoughts.

"Like what?"

"What did she look like?"

"What did she look like?" she repeated. "Wasn't very tall. Short dark hair. She must have cut it herself, that's what it looked like. I imagine she had a cute figure, though you'd never know from the clothes she wore." DeDe paused abruptly. Something else had occurred to her. "It's funny, you know. At a glance, Elsbeth looked sweet and innocent, almost naive. If you looked in her eyes, though, there was something about her. Strange, I don't know how to describe it. She could seem vulnerable and at the same time indestructible. That doesn't make sense, does it." After a moment's hesitation, she said, "I know what it was. She always seemed so emotionless, except after her father died."

"She was upset?"

"No. That's just it. She wasn't. After all those years of caring for him, you'd think she'd be devastated. He had been her sole purpose for existing. She didn't cry or anything. At least not that I saw. You know what it was? She was angry. She looked mad. She seemed full of hate. Like she had been cheated of something."

Of a life, I thought.

• • •

"After leaving the rental agent," I told Stranahan, "I went back to the house where Elsbeth and her father had lived. I canvassed the neighbors. They all said that Elsbeth and Latham were quiet and kept to themselves. The only thing the neighbors didn't agree on was Elsbeth's mother. Some said they thought she had died and that's what caused Latham's drinking. Some had heard that she had deserted them when Elsbeth was a little girl, and that's what caused Latham's drinking. Others said she had divorced Latham because of his drinking. Take your pick."

Stranahan unwrapped a stick of gum, folded it in half, and put it in his mouth. "You remember the address?" he asked.

I shook my head. "It's in the glove compartment of Loftus's car."

Stranahan glanced at Stokesberry. Stokesberry volunteered to get the address from the car. After Stokesberry had left the interrogation room Stranahan said, "He's not a bad cop. He just gets a little nervous around me." He rolled the gum wrapper into a little ball. "So you didn't find Elsbeth?"

"No. That took two days. That's all Loftus would pay for. So I drove back. As soon as I reached Broward County I was pulled over by BSO. Something about suspicion of murder. Imagine my surprise."

"Imagine." Stranahan stood up and stretched. He began pacing slowly, without the exaggerated swagger of the typical cop. He stopped in front of the two-way mirror, turned toward me, and leaned against it.

"You know what bothers me, Rice?"

"It's too pat?"

"Besides that. I don't understand why you'd agree to work for Loftus after your experience with those two."

I shrugged. "I'm just a good Samaritan who wants to see justice done."

Something that resembled a smile slithered across Stranahan's lips.

"You know what bothers me?" I could see that Stranahan really cared, so I said, "Wade Loftus left the Sand Bar about eleven-thirty in the morning. And I'm supposed to be the last person who saw him. You're trying to tell me that no one saw him all afternoon?"

"That's a Stokesberry tactic," Stranahan admitted. "He thinks it'll rattle the suspect. Actually, we have Loftus traced as late as seven Sunday evening. Apparently he and his wife quarreled and Loftus left their apartment. A neighbor across the hall confirms that."

"Mrs. Robinette."

Stranahan nodded. "She says she saw Wade Loftus leave. About a half hour later she heard Mrs. Loftus leave."

"At seven o'clock I was halfway to Saint Augustine."

"Yeah, you probably were."

"You don't really suspect me, do you?"

"We'll check your story. But no, I don't. Like you say, it's too pat. Loftus attacks you in public. You threaten to kill him. A couple days later he turns up dead in your car. You're found driving his car. I might buy that on a half-hour cop show. Of course, I don't buy your story, either."

I gave him my chagrined look. "I've told the truth."

"Probably. I'm talking about what you haven't told."

"Who, me?"

"Yeah, you. Stokesberry would interrogate you all

night for the same results we already have. I know you're not going to tell us any more. For your sake, I hope you're not holding back any material information."

"I can't think of anything."

"No? You didn't know your client was smuggling guns?"

"I knew he was a collector. Besides, I thought importing guns was legal. Why would he have to smuggle guns into the country?"

"Out of the country," Stranahan said. "He was exporting guns, which happens to be illegal without State Department licenses. Which he didn't have."

So that's what that little scene in Port Everglades was all about. Wade Loftus wasn't selling drugs to crew members. He was selling guns.

That was another piece of information I kept to myself. All I said was, "I never would have thought him clever enough to smuggle guns."

"You don't have to be a genius to smuggle guns out of this state. The NRA has wet dreams over Florida. There are no restrictive gun laws here. Permits are not required to purchase a weapon. No background checks, names aren't even run through NCIC. The only requirement to buy a gun in this state is a Florida ID, which you can buy at one counter and then buy a gun at the next counter."

"I thought there was a three-day cooling-off period in some counties."

"Big deal. Even drug dealers have to wait for their orders to be filled."

I knew what Stranahan was saying was true. Florida had become a major source of guns for the Caribbean Basin. Florida-bought guns were turning up daily in places like Colombia, Jamaica, Suriname, Guyana, and even New York. Drug cartels and Latin American rebels were willing to pay four times the purchase price. A tidy profit.

"We're not talking BB guns either," Stranahan said. "Some places in this state, you can legally walk into a gas station and buy an Uzi, a MAC-Ten and a semiautomatic pistol."

I didn't have to ask why the politicians didn't change the state laws. I knew the answer. In a business that profitable, a lot of money was changing hands. All it took was just a few bucks in the right pockets. Tallahassee pockets.

I looked at Stranahan. "You think Loftus's murder was related to his gun smuggling?"

"Could be. It's a competitive business."

twenty-one

• • • • • • • • • • • • • •

It was nearly nine P.M. by the time I was unarrested. My car was still impounded, being dissected by the lab techs. I helped myself to Loftus's Volvo. The tank was half full. I was running on empty, having not eaten all day. I drove to Cuban Frankie's.

I sank into a booth, thinking about gunrunning attorneys. I didn't have to count on my fingers to add it up. If on the average Wade Loftus bought a gun for three hundred dollars and sold it for four times that amount, he could have cleared an excess of a hundred thousand dollars a year just by selling ten guns a month. A healthy income for moonlighting. If dabbling was all he was doing. And if he was, then it wasn't likely that the major exporters would concern themselves with some small mom-and-pop smuggling operation. Not to the extent that they would kill a lawyer and draw attention to themselves. Of course, it could have been a dissatisfied buyer that wasted old Wade—there had been that altercation with the crew members in Port Everglades.

Suppose, though, that Loftus wasn't self-employed. What if he had been fronting for someone else? Who would question a gun-collecting lawyer for buying three Uzis with every fill-up at the Gas & Guns minimart? But who needed a front in Florida? The state didn't care who bought guns. Was this the Cruz connection? Were these the guns Cruz was telling me to forget?

Like a magic wand, a chilled bottle of beer appeared before my very eyes.

"You looked like you could use one," said a concerned Connie.

I said, "That's not all I could use."

• • •

Nick didn't seem surprised to see me when I walked into the Sand Bar.

"The police are looking for you," he said matter-of-factly, as if it was a daily occurrence that I was sought for questioning for the commission of unnatural acts against men, women, children, and four-legged beasts.

I took a stool at the bar. "I know. I just came from there."

"Everything copacetic?"

"For the moment."

"You going to tell me about it?"

"Sure."

"Beer?"

"That sounds good."

He nodded. "You look like you could use one."

"So I've been told."

Nick set me up with a cold long-neck and then moved down the bar to refill an empty glass for a young woman with sun-bleached bangs. Her date was propped against the jukebox, the heels of his hands pressing on the edges as he studied the playlist. At a window table sat an unfamiliar couple drinking draft beer and holding hands. A quiet evening, typical for an off-season weeknight.

The bar phone rang. Nick moseyed by like a veteran gunfighter summoned to another round of shoot-'em-up.

"Sand Bar," he answered. He looked over at me. When he was sure I was listening he said, "No, I haven't seen Harry. Right. I'll give him the message."

He hung up. Nick opened one of the drawers under the bar. He sifted through the contents and withdrew a couple newspaper clippings. He placed the articles in front of me.

"Guess who's been calling," he said.

I glanced at the clippings. They were the local press accounts of Loftus's murder. It was the byline that my eyes focused on.

"Shit," I muttered. "That was Alden Wooley on the phone?"

Nick nodded.

Over the din of muted bar talk, I scanned the articles. I didn't see anything that I hadn't already been told. The body was found in the trunk of a car. The press was discreet enough to tell their readers only that it was my car. The car, my car, had been found in the parking lot of the law offices of Loftus, Schmuck & Whiplash. The body had been discovered early Monday morning because of a puddle of blood that had dripped through the rust holes in the trunk. Loftus had been stabbed a couple times, according to the first article. The follow-up said he had died from multiple stab wounds. Give the press enough time and it would have Wade Loftus being fed through a shredder.

I drank the beer and told Nick the story. I said I was tired. I was going to go home and go to bed.

I got as far as the alley.

twenty-two

....

The red Corvette gleamed ominously in the moonlight, like Vampira's ticket to ride. The ice-woman cometh.

The car was empty.

I listened for predatory footsteps, but heard only night sounds that blended into a cacophony of evil laughter, as if the joke was on me. I heard the sound of water rippling in a nearby motel pool as someone swam after hours at his own risk. I heard the coughing and choking of cheap air conditioners. I heard television racket. I heard the nocturnal jubilee of the pedestrians on the Broadwalk. I heard common sense echoing in the dark before tapering into a parody of logic. But I heard no footsteps.

I was beginning to feel like a condemned man awaiting a dance at the executioner's ball. Where was my date?

Then I saw her face. It materialized like a bodiless apparition. A floating face, almost talcum white, with iridescent vermilion lips. She took a small step toward me. I could see her wild hair, blacker than the Marlboro Man's lungs. As she continued to edge closer to me I saw that she was wearing an indigo body stocking. Her small breasts were barely hidden by the sheer fabric, which clung to her mounds and disappeared into her recesses.

She stopped about ten feet from me, her legs spread, her arms akimbo. Her lips parted like the Red Sea into a seductive smile.

"Harry."

"Working an all-nighter?" I said.

We stared at each other, as if we were sizing up one another like ring opponents in Madison Square Garden.

She took a step closer. I recalled the last time we had met in the alley, the night I tasted my own blood. When beauty is the beast, circle the wagons.

I held up a hand. "That's close enough."

"*Pobrecito*," Carmen whispered. "Do I scare you?"

"Hell yes, you scare me." I was no macho Latino.

She smiled. But at least she kept her distance. She spread her arms and wantonly swirled, as if she was offering me access to her core.

"You like?" she said in a sultry voice.

Did I like? She looked like my next wife.

I said, "Are you here on business?"

"You think you are in danger?"

"You're forgetting, I'm the one with the mouthful of stitches."

She cast a sidelong glance at me. "I am sorry." She sounded like she meant it.

"Yeah, well, sorry doesn't butter the biscuit, baby. Sorry don't walk the dog." I was trying to sound like a movie detective in one of those old noir films.

I asked, "Did you kill Wade Loftus?"

She gave me a puzzled look. "Do you think I killed him? Is that what you think?"

It wasn't. I didn't really believe it was her style. I told her so.

"Is this what you told the police?"

Good ol' Milton Brantferger. He had taken my advice and was following me and reporting his findings. I had to admit he was good. I had forgotten all about him and hadn't caught him tagging along. There were too many shadows and niches to hide in, in the alley. I'm sure he was there. I would have said hello, but I didn't want to blow his cover. I hoped Milton had enjoyed his scenic tour of Jacksonville and surrounding areas.

"Ask the police," I said.

She looked at me chillingly. "I'm asking you, Harry."

The lady was accustomed to having her way.

"Okay," I said, "I'll tell you what you want to know, then I walk away and never see you again. Nothing personal. You tell Mundo, if he has any messages for me in the future, he sends a telegram. *Comprende?*"

Carmen shrugged. "I only deliver messages. I do not negotiate."

"Good. It's not negotiable. Deliver the message."

She nodded. "Did you tell the police about Mundo?"

"No."

She looked at me skeptically. "Did the police ask about Mundo?"

"No. Why should they?"

"Where have you been?"

They knew damn well where I had been, courtesy of Milton Brantferger. They just didn't know what I had been doing in Jacksonville and Saint Augustine.

"I've been out of town. I was working on another case. As your boss so graciously requested, I have forgotten about the guns. I have honored our agreement."

"You were working for the dead man?"

"Yes."

"The police think you killed him?"

"I don't know what the police think. But that's what they questioned me about."

Carmen's green eyes studied my face.

"What were you doing for the dead man?" she said.

"I was looking for a girl."

"What girl?"

"A go-go girl. A naked dancer. She dances under the name Lola. At least she did the last I heard. By now she could be using another name. She has a blue owl tattoo on her inner thigh."

"That's all you were doing? You were just looking for this girl Lola, and not the guns?"

"That's all I was doing."

"Did you find her?"

"No."

"And you did not mention Mundo or me to the police?"

"No."

Carmen didn't say anything. I couldn't read her thoughts. I couldn't tell if she doubted me or if she believed me. What was unsettling, though, was that her eyes were devoid of any emotion. They were like green ice.

"Nothing to the police?" she repeated. She was trying to anticipate any other questions that Cruz would ask her.

"Carmen, Mundo never came up," I assured her.

"This is true?"

"Believe it."

"If you lie . . ." She let it trail off. I was quite capable of filling in the blanks.

The melodrama starring the sweetheart of Mundo Chi and me ended shortly after midnight. We went our separate ways.

I went home.

I couldn't sleep. I was depressed. Life-and-death encounters in dark alleys tend to affect me that way.

I needed to talk. I was in dire need of a friend. My friend. Mali.

The more I thought about her, the more I missed her. Why hadn't I called her? Was I punishing her because she was having trouble shaking Chuckie's shadow? Or was I punishing myself? I should have been helping Mali by being more supportive, patient, and understanding. I had lost one woman to death. I had no choice. I didn't want to lose another woman to a bad memory. I didn't want to lose Mali because I was pigheaded. And stubborn, I've been known to be. It comes naturally.

I called her at one A.M. No answer. I remembered Carla saying something about Mali going out of town and calling me when she got back.

There was so much I wanted to say to her. I wasn't sure exactly what, but I needed to talk to her. It's a shame I had to see her with another man to understand that.

Things had to change. It couldn't keep going this way. Now that I was finally done with Wade and Eloise and company, I was going to get my priorities in order. Starting with Mali. I had to be more sensitive to her feelings. And maybe, just maybe, it was time to quit ignoring my own needs.

twenty-three

....

"What are you eating?"

"Potato chips."

"For breakfast? You're crazy."

"Who told?"

"I'm serious, Harry. What kind of diet are you on? Don't you cook?"

"Carla, I've been in my house five years and I still don't know where the kitchen is."

We were in the Sand Bar. I had come in early to inventory the paper goods. Carla arrived an hour ahead of schedule, as she often did. She liked to start the day with a swim. She disappeared into the ladies' room.

Plenty of cocktail napkins, plastic stirrers, and cardboard coasters.

Carla came out of the ladies' room wearing three strategically placed, black pirate eye-patches. It was the bikini I would have picked out for her given the chance.

"Go for a swim?" she said, draping a towel over her shoulder.

I was tempted. There was still more than an hour before we opened. But the gods were not sympathetic that morning. Standing outside, waiting for Carla to open the door, was Alden Wooley, the self-ordained journalist-laureate of Broward County. This was not going to be the day I'd intended.

Carla and Alden exchanged smiles as she walked past him. Alden caught the door before it closed. He rustled into the bar like the opening act of the Wayne Newton Follies. He reeked of Old Spice and was decked out in a Magnolia Textile Laboratories wardrobe—topped by a white fedora.

"Top of the morning, suds merchant," Alden sang, like a karaoke junkie in search of a fix.

"Jeez, Alden, I'd really appreciate it if you wouldn't waltz in here in your Truman Capote getup. You'll give the bar the wrong image."

"Splendid," he chuckled. "Your savage wit is as sharp as ever. Is that how you killed Wade Loftus?"

"Alden, I'm serious."

He seemed genuinely shocked. "My clothes offend?"

"Your clothes are fine if you're on your way to a Steve and Eydie concert, or if you're going caroling in the woods where no one can see you."

"And when did we become a fashion-conscious snob?"

"When you walked in. At least I'm dressed for the beach." Which meant a navy blue T-shirt with a white Sand Bar logo, beige canvas shorts, and deck shoes. No socks. No briefs. No errors. It was a fashion statement that was long overdue.

"Yes, well," Alden began as he sat on a bar stool across from me, "it's obvious you've been consulting alcohol for your fashion tips."

"Drink?" I said by way of a truce.

"An entrancing thought. A mimosa would be nice. Lord, it's hotter than São Paulo in December." He produced a handkerchief and patted his forehead. "We've a new den mother at the paper. Her claim to fame is that she was a B-movie queen forty years ago. She still dresses like she's in front of the cameras, and insists that we do likewise. Actually, she looks more like the star of one of those Japanese giant-reptile pictures. Her makeup must be an inch thick. She's unquestionably the most sensuous creature of this century, with the possible exception of Broderick Crawford. Here! What's this?"

"This is a beer. I asked if you wanted a drink, not what you wanted."

Lifting the glass, he said, "Then I presume I'm a guest of the house."

"It's on the house," I confirmed.

"How wonderful," he said.

"What brings you to the beach?" As if I didn't know.

"The same as you, avoiding welfare."

He took another swallow of beer and resumed. "Pressing matters. Time waits not for the newsman. If the news isn't in the next edition, it's no longer news. Harry, my boy, how I wish I could savor the rest and relaxation of ordinary occupations. How I envy you."

"Give it a rest. What's with you? Do all reporters share such an inflated opinion of their occupational worth?"

"Self-aggrandizement is an occupational necessity." He blotted his chin with a napkin. "Despite your consuming criticism of the press, can I assume you've emerged from never-never land long enough to read my accounts of the murder?"

"Oh? Was there something in the paper?"

"Exceedingly droll, I'm sure. Perhaps if you became acquainted with pages other than the sports section—"

"There's that."

"—you might find yourself better served having imbibed the words of Alden Wooley."

"I read your piece."

"Pieces," he corrected.

"Pieces," I repeated. "Thanks for the publicity."

"I cover for no man," he said pompously, even for him.

"Come down from the mount before your nose begins to bleed."

His eyebrows arched. "From the altitude, or the implied violence?"

"Pick it."

"A primitive pun."

"Change stations already. What do you want?"

"An exclusive with the erstwhile author of the murder."

"Me?"

He nodded.

I shook my head. "Forget it." I had condemned the entire experience and was taking bids from memory-demolition teams.

"Fine," Alden replied cheerfully. "I offered."

He acquiesced too quickly and too blatantly. Subtlety was not in Alden's armament. He knew I would be suspicious if he gave up without putting my protests in a hammerlock.

"Just like that?" I said.

"Just like that."

"You're willing to forget your exclusive?"

"I didn't say that. I have my exclusive. It's already written."

"Based on what?"

"Yes," he said thoughtfully. "You'd be entitled to wonder that. It is based on a few facts and a lot of supposition."

"Supposition."

"Alas, it's all I have."

"You're going to print a story based on supposition?"

"Why not?"

"It wouldn't be factual."

"But it would be news."

"Whatever happened to journalistic integrity?"

Alden shrugged. "Never heard of it."

"Obviously not. I'm glad all reporters don't think like you."

"My goodness, Harry. Do you have an inflated opinion of our occupational worth? Isn't that what you called it?"

Score one for Alden.

He fished a cigarette from his pocket. As he lighted it he stared at me through the smoke with narrowed eyes.

"Stalemate?" he said.

I picked up his empty beer mug and refilled it. I sat it in front of him and then poured myself a beer.

"Wade Loftus was smuggling guns," I said.

"Old news."

"You got something I don't, Alden?"

"Harry, I have a piece of the jigsaw puzzle that's going to help you solve the murder."

"I'm not trying to solve a murder."

"Do forgive, but I believe you will with a more conventional inducement," Alden said confidently.

"And that would be?"

Alden looked at me and smiled. "Money."

Convention is good.

"It'll depend on the deal," I said. "What is it you want?"

"The front page. Who done it."

"It'll cost you."

I had worked with Alden Wooley before I bought the Sand Bar. As an investigative reporter who didn't investigate, he used to hire me to be his ghost investigator. He paid me out of his expense account. Since I had bought the bar I had worked for Alden on only one other occasion.

"As you well know," Alden reminded me, "the paper provides me with a generous expense account for my prodigious investigative skills."

"Which I provide."

"Which is also our secret."

"What other secrets do we have, Alden?"

"Wade Loftus was stealing big-time from his partners in the law offices where he set up shop."

twenty-four

●●●●●●●●●●●●●●●●●

The gospel according to Alden Wooley:

Ira Levy and Marlon Clark were the two attorneys who shared common business expenses with Wade Loftus. They were not a firm. Three independent, self-employed lawyers splitting costs for office space, phone lines, utilities, a receptionist, and a bookkeeping service.

The alliance was formed five years ago. At that time the Three Soliciteers signed a two-year agreement with Pennekamp Bookkeepers. The service took care of billings, depositing checks in the appropriate accounts, issuing checks to creditors, and other financial transactions. When the contract with Pennekamp was about to expire, Wade Loftus suggested that other bookkeeping services be invited to submit bids. While acknowledging that Pennekamp had provided satisfactory service, Loftus maintained that he wasn't convinced that Pennekamp's fees were competitive. Levy and Clark agreed to entertain bids, meeting their specifications, as long as Loftus did the legwork. Clark didn't have the time. Levy didn't have the inclination.

In time, Loftus presented three new bids to Ira Levy.

Two of the bids were close to what Pennekamp was charging. The third quotation was about twenty-five percent less than what Pennekamp charged. Levy was in favor of accepting the lower bid, provided Pennekamp Bookkeepers was given the right of refusal to match the lower bid. Pennekamp refused, stating that the bid was ridiculously low and they would be operating at a loss if they agreed to such a figure. With Levy satisfied, Loftus approached Marlon Clark.

Clark was skeptical of the low bid. You get what you pay for and all that sort of argument. Clark didn't want to sacrifice quality to save pennies. Loftus proposed a trial period. Clark was amenable.

So Wade Loftus negotiated a five-year agreement with an escape clause. During the first six months of the agreement, if any lawyer was dissatisfied with the service for any reason, the contract could be terminated. If the six-month probationary period was successfully completed, the contract with Tigertail Bookkeeping would become indelible.

As it was, Tigertail passed muster.

During the first year of the Tigertail contract, despite inflation the lawyers all saved money, due in large part to the lower bookkeeping fee. The second year, rising costs were no longer offset by the lower fee. Ira Levy started to become disenchanted with Tigertail. Levy complained to Clark, but Clark was too busy practicing law and operating a bulk-food store to be bothered with Levy's whining. Levy began to question Wade Loftus about Tigertail. Loftus shrugged it off and said everything was costing more. Loftus suggested that Levy pass on the higher costs to his clients. Levy could live with that.

• • •

Alden paused in the midst of his epic soliloquy to light a cigarette.

I said, "I think I know where this is going. Was Wade Loftus getting a kickback from Tigertail?"

Alden inhaled deeply, his eyes riveted on me. That meant he was going to tell me something he was sure would shock me, and he didn't want to miss my reaction. Alden continued sucking on the menthol cigarette. I watched the burning tobacco crawl back toward the filter. I knew I couldn't rush Alden's little drama.

"Kickback," Alden said as he expelled smoke from his lungs. "That would indeed be an alarming discovery, were it true." Slowly he began to rock back and forth on the bar stool, like a hard-boiled Humpty-Dumpty.

Alden hacked a smoker's cough, and then with an all-knowing smirk he confided, "Harry, my boy, Wade Loftus was Tigertail Bookkeeping."

• • •

The beauty was in the subtlety. By paying Tigertail, Levy and Clark were actually paying Loftus to take care of the shared business expenses. Slowly, to not arouse suspicion, all expenses—rent, utilities, receptionist's salary, office supplies, everything—were eventually paid from Clark and Levy's accounts. Even Loftus's and Eloise's leased automobiles were unwittingly being paid for by Clark and Levy. Wade Loftus paid for nothing. Tigertail also negotiated a new cleaning contract, from which Loftus did receive a kickback.

• • •

"What a piece of work," I said. "In essence, Clark and Levy were paying Loftus to steal from them." I thought about that for a second. I guess in the end that's what we pay most lawyers to do. "How come Levy and Clark didn't notice anything?"

"Simple. Tigertail was billing Clark's and Levy's clients about ten percent more than it was supposed to," Alden explained.

"Illegal," I said, "and clever."

"Inspired. Clark represented several high rollers. They probably never even noticed."

"And," I said, "if a client did complain, all Tigertail had to do was adjust the bill and claim it was a billing error."

"Which would seldom happen. Most people won't chart a course through the devilish intricacies of an itemized bill."

"What?"

"Most people pay their bill without looking."

"It's frightening to find out I'm part of the moral majority."

"Don't expect the moral majority to rejoice from this bilious news."

"As long as I get to keep my Jerry Falwell secret decoder ring," I said. "So how did you find out that Wade Loftus was Tigertail?"

"Reveal the source that trustingly unbosomed themselves about being shamefully duped? Only a vile newsman with a watered-down ethicality and a synthetic code of honor would reveal a source."

"Levy and Clark, huh? So how did they find out they had been shamefully duped?"

"From the receptionist with the silky hair the color of caviar. At the behest of the aggrieved widow, the receptionist was packing the deceased inmate's belongings in cartons when she discovered the Tigertail booty in one of the file cabinet drawers. The late Loftus was using a P.O.

box for Tigertail's mailing address. She found Tigertail stationery and a set of double-entry books. It was all there, everything but the stolen avocados."

"Ah!" I said. "I understand now. You want me to find the stolen avocados and steal Katharine Hepburn's secret recipe for guacamole."

Alden pouted. I took advantage of his silence and told him about Loftus's firing me before Eloise had hired me, and that everything else connected to the Loftuses had been ass-backwards ever since. I told Alden about Loftus's falling in love with and wanting to marry a nude dancer young enough to be his daughter. I told him about the Loftus apartment being burglarized after Wade and Lola had played house. I told him about the antique gun collection and about Loftus selling off some of the guns that had been reported stolen, in preparation for his great escape.

That piqued Alden's curiosity.

"Escape from what?" he muttered.

"His marriage."

Alden cheered up when I told him about Carmen's knife in my mouth, and his eyes brightened when he heard how I was shanghaied by the guy in the blue *guayabera* who worked for Mundo Cruz.

Alden asked what the Cruz connection was.

"I don't know," I said. I told Alden what I was about to tell him wasn't for publication. He didn't like it, but he agreed. From our past association, I knew I could trust him. "Cruz told me to forget about the guns. I assumed he meant the antique gun collection, and he may have. But that was before I knew Loftus was exporting guns illegally. So how Cruz is connected to Wade Loftus, I still don't know. Obviously, Cruz can afford better lawyers, so I don't think theirs was an attorney-client thing. Whatever it was, Cruz got sloppy. If he hadn't hauled me in, there'd still be nothing to link him with Loftus. Cruz gave me the connection, he just didn't tell me what it was. He even paid me to forget, which I did. Only it's Cruz who won't let go. He sent Carmen to see me again last night, which further ties Cruz to Loftus. Then I'm still left with Wade Loftus repeatedly denying that he knew Cruz. Granted, Loftus wasn't an altar boy. He lied about how he met Lola, or Elsbeth. But when he hired me to find Elsbeth he still denied knowing Cruz, when there was no apparent reason for him to lie."

I wrapped up by recounting my discussion with Detectives Stranahan and Stokesberry. In between all that, I slipped in my indiscretion with Eloise Loftus.

"Sounds like you and Levy had the same motive for killing Wade Loftus," Alden said. "Rumor has it that Levy and Eloise Loftus were riding each other like a carousel. We seem to have a cornucopia of suspects."

That we did. Clark and/or Levy because Loftus was stealing from them. Levy because he wanted Eloise. Or was Loftus killed because of his gunrunning activities? Those were some scurrilous-looking characters he had met with in Port Everglades. Was Loftus killed because he had trouble remembering he was married, or because he was going to leave his wife? A crime of passion? Was there an unhappy client who had been burned by Loftus's lawyer tactics? Enough to kill? Who were his clients? What about Lola? Had she been setting up Loftus for the big sleep? Why the false addresses in Jacksonville and Saint Augustine? What about her accomplices in the burglary? It seemed the more I learned about Wade Loftus, the more suspects and motives there were.

"Who turned Loftus from attorney to cadaver?" Alden said. "That is the focus of our investigation."

"Our investigation?"

"I misspoke. Your investigation."

"Maybe. I'm still not sure I want to do this."

"Of course you do. There's the money."

"I have money."

"To prove your innocence."

"I don't have to prove it."

"To clear your name on the front page."

He had sweetened the pot. My name had been impli-cated in the murder, courtesy of the daily press. Not good publicity for a working investigator. Nor my bar, for that matter.

Seizing the moment, Alden added, "Identify the killer and you go on page one. Not only cleared, but heroically so. The publicity would bring new clients, new wealth. Think about it." Alden stood up and put on his hat. "I have a public to enlighten."

"Tell me something," I said. "How did you get Levy and Clark to admit to being so easily taken by Loftus?"

Alden hesitated in the door. He was torn between re-vealing a trade secret and missing an opportunity to brag.

"Power of the press," he said. "I told Clark I would refer to him as 'prominent attorney Marlon Clark.' Also, I promised that if he told me everything I would be able to clear his name when I reported the story."

"Clear him of what?"

"Who knows? Did you ever meet anyone who wasn't guilty of something? Happy hunting."

• • •

That afternoon Al and Irma had lunch at the Sand Bar. Al asked me why I killed Wade Loftus. Irma told him to be still. They found the body in his car, Al reminded her. Hush, said Irma, and then she told me she wanted to in-troduce me to her hairdresser's daughter.

"She's real cute. A little overweight. Only two kids,"

Irma said, making it sound like only two birthmarks. "Her name is Candy Bernstein."

"Candy Bernstein?" Al repeated. "That sounds like a Jewish dessert."

That afternoon, after I finished taking inventory— according to my count, I had too much of this and not enough of that; nothing jibed with my figures, but it was close enough—I had the stitches removed from my lip. With practice, the doctor said, I'd still be able to do my Elvis sneer.

And that afternoon I called Mali's. This time I got a recording. The number had been disconnected at the owner's request.

Disconnected. Get the message, Harry? You've been disconnected.

Lucky for me, it was Nick's day off and my night to work the bar. Just the prescription I needed. I needed to work the bar. I was in just the right mood. I hated people in love, full ashtrays on nightstands, poetry, postcards, pink wine, violins, and tablecloths. I needed to avoid intelligent forms of life. I was primed to serve the public.

The evening crowd consisted of two guys consoling a third going through a divorce, an off-duty cop with a regular on-duty divorcee, and two tourist types wearing "Hollywood, Florida" T-shirts.

I set my mind on numb, my motor skills on automatic. I poured drinks. They drank. I didn't. They talked. I didn't. They didn't listen. I did.

Excerpts from bar talk:

"Tomorrow morning we'll go back to Ocean World."

"Is that near the Galleria mall?"

"The laws are all stacked in the woman's favor."

"Harry, can we get another white wine and a Miller's?"

"Do you like Cat Stevens?"

"Can't stand him. Hank Jr. is more my style. Ever been to the Long Branch in Davie?"

"Who wants the divorce? You or her?"

"I don't know. Both of us, I guess."

"Yeah, but who initiated it?"

"What difference does it make?"

"Then maybe go to jai alai tomorrow night."

"The detectives don't do squat. They sit in their office and wait for the uniforms to make an arrest. Then they come out and take credit for the collar."

"Living alone has got to be better. It can't be worse. I don't think I'll ever marry again."

"Don't be like that."

"Right, Zsa Zsa."

"We need to buy something for Paula Getz. Remember when she went to Yellowstone she brought back that beautiful wall thermometer of Old Faithful for us?"

"What wall thermometer?"

"The one we gave your mother for her birthday."

"No way I'll get married again. What's the advantage to being married?"

"Well, you get laid the first three months."

"Shit, if that's true, my wife still owes me a month."

"My ex-husband used to say, you have to work the soil to reap the crop."

"No wonder you divorced him."

It was that kind of night. At closing, I hit the vodka pretty hard and tried not to think about Mali. About a disconnected phone. But that was all I thought about.

However, I did succeed in avoiding intelligent life.

twenty-five

....

Just as I segued from "A Girl Like You" *into* "Lonely Too Long," the phone started bellyaching. I let it ring itself to death while I leisurely finished my shower and my musical salute to the Rascals.

It was that time of the morning. I was feeling better than I should have, all things considered. I had consumed enough vodka after closing to take on the next Ice Age naked. And it had been another sleepless night. I had lain awake rerunning highlights from *The Best of Mali & Harry,* the lost episodes. A fantasy fest in Key West. A trip to Cross Creek. Working together on my last case.

Be still, foolish heart, you're missing the concert. "Ain't Gonna Eat My Heart Out Anymore." Nothing left to devour. It was a performance worthy of a standing ovation. If I got any better I'd have to start showering with chorus girls.

The medicine cabinet was well stocked with all kinds of bathroom paraphernalia—disposable razor, shaving cream, toothpaste, nail clippers, tweezers, unplucked magic twangers, an espresso cup, screwdriver, and scissors. It was all there. Everything but medicine. No little bottles of Love Potion Number Nine.

The phone rang. Someone was trying to connect with the disconnected.

I answered the phone.

"Thank goodness, Harry. I called a few minutes ago and there was no answer. I must have dialed the wrong number. It's been so hectic, with everything that's happened." She talked faster than the March Hare on speed. "I've been worried 'cause I haven't heard from you. I was afraid you were mad at me. When you didn't call, I wasn't sure what to think."

"Hello, Eloise."

"I have to see you. It's very important." She talked right over my greeting, never breaking stride. "If this is a good time I can come right over."

"No!" I blurted. Then, more calmly, I said, "This is not a good time."

"When, Harry? Soon. Today. This morning."

"Not today," I said firmly.

She headed me off at the period before I could say anything else. "Please, Harry. I'm frantic. Don't you turn on me, too," she pleaded.

Pleading women and shivering puppies in the rain.

"What's the problem?" I asked with the soothing voice of a Tibetan monk suffering from bleeding hemorrhoids.

"Not on the phone." Her voice said, Please.

"All right." I agreed because I prefer to conduct interviews face to face. It's too easy to lie to someone over the phone. Or be lied to.

"Should I come over?" she said.

"No. Not here."

"My apartment?"

"No." I wasn't going to be alone with this woman. I

wanted a chaperon. "I'll meet you at the Sand Bar at ten-thirty."

Poor Carla had just volunteered for bodyguard duty. If she ever found out, she would demand—and deserve—a raise.

"Thank you, Harry. I'll be there at ten-thirty."

I hung up.

Oh goody. Another fun-filled day.

• • •

At ten thirty-five A.M., Eloise Loftus was sitting across from me in the Sand Bar office. For my protection the office door was open. Carla Meadows was minding the bar. Sgt. Joe Friday and Officer Bill Gannon were working the street.

She wasn't dressed like a widow. She wore one of those peasant blouses, like Jane Russell had almost on when she posed for *The Outlaw* movie poster. Guess? jeans and Dr. Scholl's clogs completed the mourner's ensemble for the nineties.

Eloise clutched her hands as if she was a distressed maiden. I figured I was supposed to reassure her that I was still her champion. I blinked. I was sure she had rehearsed everything she was going to say, and the protracted silence was all part of the script.

She waited for me to pick up my cue. I picked up the newspaper.

"Harry, I need your help. My life is a shambles."

"Tell it to Geraldo," I said without looking up from the paper.

"You're such a shit. I ought to fire you."

I lowered the paper. "I usually get a month's severance pay."

She shot me a look that would have turned Medusa to stone.

She sighed. "Why do you insist on giving me a hard time?" Her anger was fading. "Sometimes I wish you would just leave me alone."

"Excuse me?" I said. "Lady, you called me."

"Because I'm scared, Harry. I need help. Someone is after me. You don't believe me, do you?"

"I didn't say that."

"You didn't have to. I can see it in the way you're looking at me. Harry, do I have to remind you that my condo was burglarized on my daughter's birthday? My office was broken into on Wade's birthday, and my car was stolen on our anniversary."

"Consider me reminded."

"I'm not finished. Wade was killed on my niece's birthday. Do you see?"

I stifled a laugh. "Yeah, it's clear as vodka. Your niece's birthday? Let's see if I got this. Someone is after you. Wade is murdered, but you're the injured party. I bet Wade would be relieved to know it was nothing personal. Give it a rest, Eloise. Your niece's birthday? Do you hear how ridiculous it sounds?"

She didn't hear it. "Harry, I'm being set up. The police questioned me about Wade's murder. It's almost as if they think I did it."

"They're questioning everyone. That's their job. Hell, they think *I* did it."

Her eyes widened. "The police talked to you?"

I nodded. "Interrogated me with rubber hoses and rolled-up phone books." Give the ex-clients macho. It's good for referrals.

"What did you tell them?"

"Name, rank, and truth."

"What about me? Did you talk about me?"

"Yes, Eloise, we talked about you. They wanted the sordid details of our torrid affair."

"How did they know?"

"How did they know what?"

"The affair."

"We didn't have an affair."

"You know."

"Yeah, I know, but nobody else does. Everyone seems to think we had a thing."

"Well, you don't think I gave them that impression, do you?"

"I think everyone who talks to you gets that impression. If you're not careful, you're going to make Ira Levy jealous."

Eloise's eyes flashed. She made a hissing sound and probably would have sunk her venomous fangs into me if she had been able to reach me across the desk. It began to seem less likely that Eloise Loftus would fall in love with me.

"Now that I have your attention," I said, "perhaps you'll tell me why you're really here."

twenty-six

• • • • • • • • • • • • •

"*I was on my way* to Gainesville when Wade was murdered," Eloise said. "We'd been arguing most of the afternoon." She sat quietly for a moment, letting her thoughts drift back. "It was the same argument we had been having for almost five years. He started it about six months after we were married. He wanted me to sell my condo. He said he was the only one that had made compromises for the marriage. He said he had given up his way of life, his home, to marry me and I hadn't given up anything. Do you believe that? He didn't think it was a compromise to let him move into my home?"

I didn't say anything.

Eloise took a deep breath. "Just because he gave up his home he thought I should give up mine. He wanted us to find a place together, one that would be 'ours.' He said whenever we disagreed I acted like I resented him, as if he were a guest in my home who had overstayed his welcome. It was how I tried to control him, he said. It was all nonsense."

She stared at her hands for a long moment, then said, "What did he know about compromise? That stupid gun collection of his. You think I enjoyed those silly gun shows and NRA arguments?" She looked up at me. "Beware of collectors, Harry. It's about the depth of their character."

I didn't say anything.

"We argued about . . . We argued about the girl. And other things. Wade just wanted to argue. Maybe he thought if I was miserable enough I would agree to a no-fault divorce. Well, there was no chance of that." She was becoming more intense as she rambled on. "He was the lawyer. I knew if that was what he wanted, it meant that was the most advantageous for him." She smirked. "Wade used to tell me stories about things attorneys would do, things that sounded unethical at best. I would ask him if that was legal and he would answer, 'Let's just say it's not illegal.' "

She shook her head. "I know how I sound. And I know it wasn't all his fault. We hardly knew each other when we married. How well can you know someone after several months? It was like buying a car under bright lights. Everything was so shiny and perfect on the surface. Six months into the marriage, the flaws appear. I knew it then. Maybe Wade did, too. That's when he started to complain about finding a place that would be 'ours.' That's when he first accused me of trying to control him. I suppose neither one of us wanted to admit that we had made a mistake. Which was a bigger mistake. By sticking our heads in the sand, a six-month mistake became a five-year mistake. Those are years I'll never get back. We should have ended it then, when we first knew. You can't force people to fit where they don't belong."

We sat silently for a long time. I still wasn't sure why she was telling me all this. I wondered how prehistoric detectives dealt with ice queens.

After a while I said, "What happened the day Wade was murdered?"

She gazed pensively at me. "Like I said, we argued. We both got nasty. And loud. When Wade had had enough he walked out. That was his answer to everything. Pout and run. Oh, he'd always come back, but his act wore thin quickly. Pout and run. Well, I decided this time I wasn't going to be the dutiful wife who waits for her lord and master to return from his precious tantrum. I packed some things and took off. . . ."

She stopped, as if she had lost her train of thought.

"For Gainesville?" I prompted.

She nodded. "But I didn't get that far. I stopped at a wayside motel near Melbourne. The next morning I was more rational. I was not going to run away. I wasn't about to give Wade an abandonment argument. Actually, I had made up my mind to go home and file for divorce. I wasn't going to wait for him. When I got back to my apartment, Wade was not there. I assumed he had already gone to work. I called his office, and that was when Ira told me what had happened."

"He told you on the phone?"

"Yes."

"Sensitive guy."

"You judge everyone, don't you?" she snapped.

My response was not immediate. I thought about what she said. "I guess I deserve that."

"I guess you do."

She sat woodenly, glaring at me. I caught a whiff of the ocean air. I could visualize young couples outside, strolling hand in hand. Kids eating hot dogs, spilling relish on their chins. Oiled skin glistening in the sun. Inside, I was facing an arctic front.

Change the subject, Harry.

"Did you know your husband was smuggling guns?" I said.

She looked away. "The police told me."

"You didn't know before then?"

She shook her head. "No."

"What about Wade's clients? Do you know anything about them?"

"No. Why? Do you think it could have been a client?"

"What do you think?"

She gave that a moment's deliberation. "I suppose it's possible. I guess anyone could have done it."

"You mean like a rival suitor?"

"Damn you! Sometimes I think you forget who hired you."

"Impossible."

"Whose side are you on?"

"I don't know. How many sides are there?"

"Harry?" Carla was standing in the doorway, a welcome interruption. But then an all-expense-paid vacation to Somalia would have been a welcome reprieve. "I'm sorry to bother you. The man that was here last week— the one you left with?—is back. He insists on seeing you. He said it would only take a minute."

I looked at Eloise. She nodded. I followed Carla into the bar.

He was sitting at a window table. His hair was slicker than I-95 in the rain. The blue *guayabera* had been exchanged for a chocolate *guayabera*.

I walked over to him.

"We going cruising again?" I said.

He stood up and handed me a folded slip of paper.

I took it. "What's this?"

"A telegram."

Carmen had given Mundo Cruz my message. I glanced at the slip of paper. I unfolded the "telegram." It said, "The blue owl dances in the Promised Land."

Before I had time to decipher the cryptic message, I heard a loud gasp behind me.

"Luis!"

Luis looked over my shoulder, past me. He nodded and walked out.

I turned around. Standing with her mouth agape in the office doorway was Eloise. She did an about-face and disappeared into the office. I joined her.

"You know him?" I said.

"What was he doing here?" she said with a perplexed innocence.

"You answer me first," I said with an authority I didn't have. "How do you know him?"

Eloise sighed, like an exhausted combatant in a lovers' quarrel. "He works for my godfather."

I sank into my chair, dumbfounded.

"Mundo Cruz?" I said.

She nodded.

"Mundo Cruz is your *padrino*?" I still couldn't believe it.

"Yes. No. Not like that. He's my baptismal godfather."

"I don't believe this." The woman was exasperating. "Jesus, no wonder Hindu detectives only solve cases in their former lives. What the . . . Why didn't you tell me this before, when I told you that Mundo Cruz had told me to butt out?"

She shrugged.

"Did you put him up to that?" My tone was accusatory.

"No. No, I was shocked when you told me." She was adamant. "I don't know how or why he got involved."

"How did you—"

"My father," she interrupted. "He worked for Mundo years ago, on Mundo's yacht. When I was sixteen my parents were killed in an auto accident. I was in boarding school. Mundo continued paying for my education.

He took care of me until I married. Over the years we've stayed in touch. Christmas cards. Birthdays, we call. Maybe once a year Mundo invites me to lunch to see how things are."

"When was the last time you spoke to him?"

"Last summer. We had dinner at the Forge."

"Was this after your apartment was hit?"

"Yes."

"So he knew about the gun collection?"

"Yes. I told him. Why all these questions about Mundo? Do you think he killed Wade?"

I certainly hoped not.

I said, "Did Wade know about you and Mundo?"

She shook her head. "I never told him."

"Why?"

"I'm not sure. A wife doesn't tell a husband everything. And Wade being a lawyer, it might upset him if he knew my godfather had a somewhat suspect past."

"Well," I said, "at least Wade told the truth about something."

"What was Luis doing here?" Eloise still wanted to know.

The blue owl dances in the Promised Land.

I thought about that and said, "I don't know."

"I should have expected that," she said disgustedly, as if I had tricked her into showing me hers and now I wouldn't show her mine.

I looked at her. "Eloise, don't expect anything from me."

She looked hurt. "You mean you're not going to help me?"

That would take an army of analysts, but that's not what I said.

"I'm going to look for Wade's killer, if that's what you

want to know," I told her. "I was working for your husband when he died. Maybe I owe it to him. Maybe I just want to clear my name with the police. If that helps you, fine. But that's all I'm going to do."

twenty-seven

. . . .

The blue owl dances in the Promised Land?

A clear sky, a tropic breeze, and I was sitting indoors trying to solve a riddle when I could have been frolicking at the beach. Well, I was at the beach. But I wasn't frolicking. No, I was pondering imponderables like a blue owl dancing in a promised land. The blue owl was a tattoo, but what was the Promised Land?

Caricature of the detective musing.

At least I did know that Eloise Loftus was the Mundo Cruz connection. Not much of an accomplishment, though, since I still didn't understand Cruz's interests or the extent of his involvement.

Who would want to kill an unfaithful, obnoxious, woman-beating, gun-smuggling, embezzling, insurance-cheating shyster? That was the question.

The problem was, there were too many volunteers.

It was time to handicap the field. Play the odds. Start with the favorite, and through the process of elimination find the best bet.

A disgruntled client seemed like a long shot. Had Wade Loftus been a divorce lawyer, it might have been even money that a depleted and desperate ex-husband had cashed in Loftus's ticket. Still, it wouldn't hurt to have Alden Wooley work up a client list. Probably busy-work, but it couldn't be completely ignored.

Someone connected to Loftus's gun-smuggling? Another dark horse, though not necessarily a sucker's bet. He had been dealing with some unsavory characters. I just didn't have enough data. Maybe come back to this later. For the moment there were other entries that deserved more consideration.

According to Alden Wooley, Marlon Clark and Ira Levy didn't find out that Loftus was dipping into their purses until after he was murdered. So that couldn't have been a motive—if Clark and Levy were telling the truth. I had my doubts about Levy. Not just because of his rumored liaisons with Eloise—which she neither denied nor confirmed, and I knew all too well how that worked. What bothered me about Levy was that little scene that Nick and I had witnessed at the law offices. We had seen Levy storm out of Loftus's office, yelling at Loftus. Something about the Tigertail mess being Loftus's fault. Levy had threatened Loftus to the effect that Loftus had "better do something" about it.

Can't forget the weepless widow. If it was a crime of passion, Eloise would have been the prohibited favorite. Only, as near as I could tell, the Loftuses appeared to have a passionless marriage—their passions being spent in other barns. On the surface this didn't appear to be a crime of passion or a heat-of-the-moment killing. Something nagged at me, though. If it wasn't a crime of passion, and assuming Eloise had no other motive, like a life insurance bonanza, why did she go through all the trouble to tell me where she was when Loftus was murdered? Could have been perfectly innocent chatter. Could have been how she dealt with her grief. Could have been trying to salve her conscience, since their last words to each other had been heated. Could have been anything. Still, I'm suspicious of people giving me information I don't need. Why the alibi? Covering for herself? Covering for someone else? An accomplice?

Perhaps there was an unknown entry. Perhaps someone was trying to set up Eloise. Perhaps she was the ultimate victim. Perhaps there was something to the significant-date robberies. And murder. Perhaps I had discounted her fears too quickly.

The morning line would probably favor something from Mundo Cruz's stable. A professional hit made to look amateurish. Not likely. The pros do a job to make a point. They don't want any misunderstanding. Cruz was Eloise's godfather. He would not have Wade Loftus murdered in a manner that would cast suspicion on his goddaughter. Also, if Mundo Cruz was still an active bad guy, he would have been too big-time to be bothered by Loftus's little neighborhood gunrunning operation. But why did Cruz want me to stop looking for the guns, when it was Eloise who had hired me to find the collection? Was he protecting her from something? Did he know that Loftus had been selling off the collection? Then why didn't Cruz just squeeze Loftus? Maybe that's what he did.

I sat there for about ten minutes, bouncing my Cruz-as-killer hypothesis off the floor. It deflated a little with each bounce, until it was flat. I toyed with a couple scenarios that would play better in the Sunday funnies than in a courtroom.

I picked up the "telegram" and read it again. "The blue owl dances in the Promised Land."

What about Lola? Loftus wanted her found. Was she a candidate? What about her friends who had cleaned out the Loftus apartment? She hadn't been acting alone. What did Elsbeth know? What could Lola tell me? What did a naked dancer with a blue owl tattoo know?

The Promised Land? What did that mean? Heaven? Was Lola dead? Was Cruz telling me that he had killed Lola?

I called the police and asked for Homicide.

"Stranahan," said Stranahan.

I told him who it was. He didn't need a reminder.

"Glad you called. You saved me the trouble. You can pick up your car at the compound. Stop by the office and I'll give you a chit to claim it. The crime scene specialists are done with it."

"So am I. I don't want it."

"Fine. Just don't leave it here. You got forty-eight hours. After that we have it towed and you start paying storage."

"I'll take care of it."

"Thought you might. Now what are you calling for? Confession's good for the soul."

"Actually, I need some information." I wasn't sure how to ask him if there had been any dead naked dancers turned in lately.

"What do you need, Rice?"

"I got this message, and I'm not sure what it means."

"What's the message?"

"The blue owl dances in the Promised Land." I didn't tell him who it was from. "I think the blue owl is a dancer I'm looking for. But I'm not sure what the Promised Land is."

"Well," Stranahan said, "it could be Canaan."

"You're getting biblical on me."

"I do that religiously. Or it could be the naked bar with that name that's always getting busted."

"Where?"

"Hialeah."

"Thanks."

"Don't mention it. I figure we owe you for the inconvenience. Your alibi checked out. You're officially a nonsuspect."

"That's reassuring."

"Don't forget your car. Oh, and you better do something about that spare tire of yours."

"The spare? It's never been used. It's a new tire."

"It's bald and it's flat," Stranahan said.

"Then Loftus must have changed tires."

"Is that right? Let me look. Hold on. Let's see. Yeah. He must have. There was a new tire on the car. Right rear. You didn't do that?"

"No."

Stranahan said, "Then he must have had a flat. That's very interesting."

"Yeah, it's fascinating," I said.

"Your voice betrays you."

"What's the big deal? He had a flat."

"And you call yourself a detective."

He hung up.

I shrugged off Stranahan's last remark as just a jibe. I called information. They had a listing for the Promised Land in Hialeah. I called the number and asked for their address. The hours were eleven A.M. to three A.M.

I dialed Nick's home number.

"Hello." He was breathing heavily.

"Are you all right?"

"Yeah. Working out."

"I got a job. If you're up for it."

"Sure. What do you need?"

"I need you to spend the afternoon watching naked women dance."

Nick was momentarily silent. "What's in it for me?"

I laughed and gave him the address of the Promised

Land. I told him we were looking for a dancer with a blue owl tattooed on her inner thigh.

"What if I find her?" he said.

"Call me."

"I'm supposed to relieve Carla behind the bar later," he reminded me.

"I know. If the dancer we want isn't on the day shift, I'll come down and check out the night dancers."

"She got a name?"

"Lola. Maybe."

"Blue owl tattoo."

"You got it. If I don't hear from you by four o'clock, I'll come down and relieve you."

"Take your time."

He hung up. Nick's not one for long good-byes.

I helped Carla behind the bar until about two. Midafternoon lull. Before I forgot about it I went back into the office and looked up Larry Wildgoose's phone number. I dialed it.

He answered with the last four digits of the number: "Two-two-seven-seven."

"Wildmon, hasn't the border patrol caught up with you yet?"

"Harry, mon! Now what you wanna say such a thing to old Lawrence for? What border patrol be wanting with me?"

"You got your green card?"

"No way, mon. Too much money."

"And taxes."

"That too."

"You still buying cars to ship to the islands?"

"Depends."

"How much you paying?"

"Depends. How hot is it?"

"It's not. It's mine. I've got the title."

"Six hundred dollars."

"You haven't seen the car."

"People don't sell me expensive cars unless they're hot."

"This one's not."

"So what you drive?"

"Ten-year-old Ford."

"Mileage?"

"Yeah, it's got mileage."

"Rust?"

"Half of it's rust-free."

"What half?"

"The upholstery."

He ho-ho'd like a department-store Santa.

"Five hundred dollars," he said.

"You bastard."

"Don't sweet-talk me, mon. We through negotiating."

"All right. But it's got to be picked up tomorrow."

"No problem."

"There could be. It's at the police compound."

"No problem. I employ a U.S. citizen."

"Chalk up one for EEO. All right," I said. "Have your citizen see Detective Stranahan to get the car released."

"I need papers."

"I'll leave the title and registration with Carla. She's one of the bartenders here."

"The Sand Bar?"

"Yeah. I'll sign them; you get them notarized. Give the money to Carla and she'll give you the papers. And Wild-goose?"

"Yeah, mon?"

"Cash."

"Bahamian?"

"U.S. Bastard."

He was ho-ho-ing when I hung up.

What next, I wondered. All I had to do was look up to find out. My heart stopped in mid-beat. Just when I thought I had lost her, there she was. Standing in the doorway with a shy smile was Mali.

twenty-eight

....

"Remember me?" she said softly. She stood in the doorway, her shoulder leaning against the jamb, her ankles crossed.

I nodded. "There's something familiar about you. Didn't you used to work at Raoul's Tanning Salon?"

Mali smiled. "You a regular at Raoul's?"

"Hey," I said. "I never had to pay for a tan in my life."

More of that smile. I was staring at her, afraid she might disappear if I took my eyes off her. Seeing her again resurrected long repressed feelings. She looked so good. She was wearing the "Coconut Grove Art Show" T-shirt that I bought her last year. A short denim skirt and leather sandals exposed her firm dancer's calves. Her face glowed with that spiritual beauty that was all Mali's and surfaced with her every smile. It made my skin tingle and my heart flutter. How do you tell that to someone?

It was strange. Mali and I had been as familiar as life-long friends. We had passed messages between us with just a glance. Yet at that awkward moment, we were as tentative as first-time lovers. I wondered if she was feeling the same subterranean nervousness that I tried to conceal behind a mask of nonchalance. I don't know what she felt. I didn't have a clue. Too often I hear people say, "I know what you're thinking." I can't do that. I never know what other people are thinking.

I wanted to run over and hug her. I guess I was waiting for her to tell me it was all right to do so. I was looking for permission. It had been a long time since there had been someone I could hold without first getting their approval. Mali and I were like that once. I missed that. I missed her.

"I've been thinking about you," she said.

That was a good sign. Maybe she had been thinking what I would have wished her to be thinking—that what we once had was too good to let go.

"I've missed you." I startled myself by saying that.

Mali stared deeply into me. "Have you?"

Something in the way she said that. Not sure that I had missed her, but wanting me to answer her. The fundamental truth? I was utterly lost without her. What did I say?

"Say, dollface, are you going to stand there all day?" I said, sounding like a cartoon Bogart. "Come in. Have a seat. Take a load off. Put your feet up. Stay awhile."

"Gee," she said. "What girl could refuse an invitation like that?"

Her walking across the room and sitting in the chair relaxed me. It was as if she had broken through some invisible barrier between us. She shifted in the chair, getting more comfortable. To stay awhile?

"How have you been?" she said.

"I don't know. I haven't seen today's newspaper. You been keeping up with my exploits?"

She nodded. "I feel guilty about recommending you to Eloise. It's so awful what's happened, and then to see you dragged into it."

I shrugged. "Goes with the turf."

"Is everything working out okay for you?"

I nodded.

"You want to talk about it?" she said.

I looked at her. "That's not why you're here, is it?" Gut feeling. Exchanging messages with just a glance.

She studied me for a moment. "No."

We sat there, looking at each other. My stomach clenched as if it had just been fed a lethal dose of Spam casserole. A premonition? I had a hunch she was in trouble. Something was bothering her. I was sorry she was troubled, yet I was pleased that when it counted, when it really mattered, she turned to me.

I wanted to tell her I would fix whatever it was, but she spoke first.

"Let me tell you what's been happening in my life lately," she began. "About four weeks ago, quite by accident, I ran into an old friend of Chuck's. His name is Phillip. I hadn't seen Phillip in over seven years. It was not long after Chuck and I split up. Phillip and I dated for a short time before we drifted in different directions."

She paused momentarily, collecting her thoughts.

"It's all right, Mali," I reassured her. Go on, tell me about Phillip the Bastard. Tell me what he's done. How he's stalked you. How you had to have your phone disconnected so he couldn't harass you. Tell Sir Harry, knight in shining armor, all of it so he can make it better for you. I want to hold you, protect you, make you happy.

"The turn of events has been so sudden. Picking up where we left off, under different circumstances, our relationship evolved to a deeper level." She spoke slowly, testing the waters.

I was as calm as a frozen lake.

She said, "I've moved in with Phillip. We're planning to marry in the very near future."

Stunned.

Instant disbelief, depression, astonishment, anxiety, panic, confusion—a myriad of emotions were on a collision course within my solar plexus.

Shocked.

I hadn't seen it coming. So much for the protective shield of self-delusion.

Shattered.

• • •

The night of the sudden and horrifying realization that Theresa was indeed going to die, I left the hospital after watching her sleep for several hours. Aimless, directionless, no place to go, I drove in a desperate stupor, trying to put distance between me and my internal chaos.

The anguish was overwhelming. The memories that wouldn't be enough, the memories that would never be. A hurt that narcotics couldn't anesthetize. An untreatable pain.

I was scared, with nowhere to run.

At three A.M. I was knocking on a door. I remembered leaving the hospital, getting in the car, and driving off. Then I was knocking on a door. I don't remember parking the car or walking up to the door. I didn't even know whose door I was knocking on.

A light came on overhead. Cat opened the door.

I stared quietly at her, though my insides were screaming. I felt empty, and yet I was full of pain and fear. I couldn't speak.

"My God, Harry," Cat whispered. "What is it?"

Again I tried to speak, but no words came out.

She reached for my hand. "Come inside."

Cat led me to the living room. We sat on the couch. She held my face between her hands and looked into my eyes.

"What is it, Harry?" She kept staring at me. "Oh, Jesus," she said softly. "Theresa?"

I breathed in deeply, trying to ward off the consuming ache. I began to shake.

Cat put one arm around my trembling shoulders. With her other hand she gently pulled my head to rest against her breast.

"It's okay. It's okay," she whispered repeatedly. "It's okay. I've got you. Go ahead, dear. I've got you. It's okay. I won't let go."

Cat held on while I cried myself to sleep.

When I woke up it was light out. I was still on the couch. And Cat was still holding on.

• • •

"Harry?" Mali said with a concerned voice. "What are you thinking about?"

The painful truth was that at that moment I was thinking, if I were to suddenly disappear there would be no one to miss me. Disposable Rice. That was my legacy.

Of course, I did not tell Mali that. That's what I do best. I don't tell people anything. I keep it to myself. If I thought that was the easy way, the safest way, I was wrong. The consequences were devastating, and would be a lot more difficult to live with than if I had just risked it and told her what I felt back when it might have made a difference. No matter what her response had been. As it was, now I would never know what might have been.

Mali was still looking at me. I weakened a little every time I looked at her. That had never changed. What was I supposed to say? There were no Cliff Notes to help me. I had to play it straight. Or fake it.

I shook my head and forced a smile. "Nothing. I'm happy for you. That's all."

Her eyes pierced me. "You all right with this?"

"What's not to be all right with?" Sophisticated chuckle. "Believe me. I'm very happy for you. Ecstatic. I want to run out and buy you a wedding gift. Are you registered at Bloomie's or Kmart?"

The humorless comedy of heartache.

Silence.

"What," I said. "What do you want from me, Mali? What do you want me to say to you?"

"I want you to tell me what you're thinking. What you feel."

"Get in touch with my feelings? Is that what you want?"

"Yes I do."

"No you don't."

"You're wrong, Harry."

"Believe me, Mali. You don't want to know."

I stared hard at her, daring her to contradict me. She was watching me, challenging me to cut loose. She won. Before I knew it, without thinking, rewriting, or editing, I let it all spill out.

"Damn it, Mali. You come waltzing in here and tell me you met some guy yesterday and you're getting married tomorrow. All right. You want to know what I think? I think it sounds like two people desperate to get married and they don't care to who. Wait a minute. Let me finish. Do you remember? It wasn't long after Cat and Dickie introduced us; about the third or fourth time we went out for dinner. I'll even tell you where it was. Saint Michel's in Coral Gables. You had crêpes and I had steak au poivre. Afterward, we took a walk to a used-book store. You knew the old man who ran it. Anyway, that night over dinner you asked me why I had never remarried. I was having trouble explaining to you, without sounding snobbish, my dread of the ordinary, the routine. And you understood. You reached across the table and held my hand. You told me I was special and I should wait for someone special. Do you remember that?"

Mali smiled and nodded.

"Well, Mali, you're special." You are so special. "And you deserve special. I hate to see you give up and settle for whatever comes along." Most of all, lady, I don't want to lose you. Things that go unsaid. "Don't do it, Mali." That I said. "Is there anything I can do or say to make you change your mind?"

At least she thought about it before saying, "No. I don't make this kind of decision lightly."

"You make it sound like a business decision."

"Do I?" she said quietly. Her eyes were sad.

I looked away. Ashamed.

"It's amazing," she said. "You can remember the tiniest detail from five years ago."

"I remember everything, Mali."

"I know you do. So do I. I haven't forgotten how you surprised me with the hand-painted photo of the ballet shoes, the one we'd seen at the Promenade. I remember the flowers you sent me from Rome. The chest of drawers you refinished for me. I remember the first time we went out, just the two of us. We went to the racetrack and then to Cap's Place. You took me to my first football game." She closed her eyes and smiled. "Most of all, Harry, I remember how you've always been there when I needed someone."

"You've been good for me, too, Mali." I wanted to tell her I was confused, that I didn't understand any of this. I said, "What is it? Is it because I don't use the 'L' word?"

She laughed. "Oh, Harry, I love you, too. I really do. I enjoy being with you. You make me laugh. You make me happy. You have a zest for life that few do. I delight in your spontaneity, the way you'll get on a plane and fly off somewhere just on a whim."

I felt like I was listening to my eulogy. "Are you saying good-bye to me?" I asked her seriously.

"Absolutely not. It's important to me to make sure you know that nothing will ever take away what I feel for you. You've been such an incredibly supportive and caring friend."

"Then why the Dear John?"

"That's not what this is."

"You know what I mean. Why the rush?"

"Harry," she said almost wistfully, "I'm thirty-six years old. I'm not a kid. I don't get offers every day."

"Mali, you're too gifted to think like that. I mean, is this what you really want? To be moored to a washer and dryer and be known as the wife of Phillip? Look, there goes Phillip's cook, Phillip's maid, Phillip's piece of ass. What about Mali? What happens to her? Is that what you want? To be someone's possession?"

"That's not fair. You don't even know Phillip."

"Neither do you," I shot back.

"He's stable, reliable, dependable."

"You just described an 'eighty-two Honda."

"I'm not going to match wits with you. Besides, you said it yourself. You shy away from habit and you cringe at the thought of routine. You don't want to live in a rut of Wednesday bridge with the neighbors, Saturday golf with the guys, and backyard barbecues with the Daughters of the American Revolution. Those are your words. Maybe you'd find the routine of marriage confining, but I think it would be comforting."

"Comforting? You're giving up. Marriage doesn't have to be like that."

She sighed. "Harry, you have a romantic's outdated idea of marriage. There are no magic carpet rides."

"I don't believe that. I was always riding high when we were together."

That broke the rhythm. Mali held her hand over mouth. When she finally spoke there was a slightly perceptible tremor in her voice. "I never knew that. You never said anything."

"Some things don't have to be said."

"Some things do."

"Would it have made a difference if I had said anything?"

She turned away for a moment, then looked forlornly at me.

"Think about it," she said. "Do you really want me to answer that?"

She was right. It was a can't-win question. There was no answer that was going to make me happy. I didn't want to know, only because I wasn't sure which answer would make me feel worse than I already did.

We went for a walk on the beach, along the water's edge. The sky was that beautiful deep blue which is indigenous to south Florida and the Caribbean islands. There was a nimble breeze coming in off the ocean, bringing with it undulating clusters of kelp, which were ultimately deposited on the shore in a saltwater foam. On the horizon was the shimmering silhouette of a solitary drift-fishing boat. That was how I felt. Like a solitary drifter.

At first our pace was brisk. When Mali took my hand in hers, I slowed us down, foolishly thinking that the slower we walked, the longer we would be together. In reality, it just meant we didn't walk as far. We strolled in the sand past the barbecue pits and redwood picnic tables shaded by the tall Australian pines. At the sea turtle refuge we cut over to the Broadwalk.

Except for the squealing and laughing of three young girls sailing a Frisbee, the beach was quiet, as it is most off-season weekday afternoons. The few pedestrians on the walk I recognized as beach regulars. There were the waitresses that worked by night and tanned by day. The overweight elderly with middle-aged desires, sitting on benches, watching young mothers wipe spilled snow cones off their preschoolers.

Walking past the Coral Rock Raw Bar, we caught the waft of deep-fried clams seeping from the screened patio. A sixties rock 'n' roll song blended with the whirring of fluttering palm fronds. Familiar sights, smells, and sounds that did nothing to constrict the expanding sensation that I was lumbering on the edge of make-believe. Denial was beginning to work. The more Mali and I walked, holding hands, the more I was convinced that she would not marry Phillip. There was no way. I would just pretend it away. I would pretend that I didn't hurt. And I would pretend that my eyes were watering because of an allergic reaction to something other than heartache. Seaweed. Yes, that was it. I would pretend that I had everything under control.

For most of the walk I selectively listened to Mali tell me about Phillip. I heard what I wanted and translated it at will. She told me about Phillip's rich uncle. Rich Uncle had several businesses in the southeast states. Rich Uncle owned a seafood restaurant in Biloxi that was managed by his sister. There was a motel in Cedar Key supervised by Phillip's son from a second marriage. Phillip managed a dive shop, dive school, and rental boat business for Rich Uncle on Key Biscayne. The whole family worked for Rich Uncle. Translated, it sounded like three generations of feverish vultures striving for the top position on Rich Uncle's hit parade of heirs. Maybe that wasn't a literal translation, but being a recent recipient of a purple heart, I felt I was entitled to a little poetic license. Especially when my Mali was being wooed by a man whose most ambitious goal was to achieve lifetime dependency on a relative's legacy.

Well, she wasn't married yet. Maybe this is what I needed to jolt some sense into me. I was determined not to lose her. Whatever it took. No exceptions. There was so much I wanted to say to her, but I shied away from it. What I had to say, needed to say, was too important to do without benefit of rehearsal. Had to hide those undisguised feelings.

As Mali and I entered the Sand Bar, Carla said, "Harry, Nick called for you over an hour ago. He said to tell you it was time to relieve him at the Promised Land. Do you know what he's talking about?"

"Yes," I said.

I turned to Mali and started to tell her I had to go.

She squeezed my hand. "It's all right," she said. "Take care of Nick."

"I know. I have to. But I—"

"We'll talk some more."

"Really?"

She smiled. "Really."

Mali hugged me. She smelled like the stars and felt like life was supposed to feel. I remembered Cat holding me, and I was afraid I was going to start crying. The sheer tenderness of the moment, the shared kindness of another person, the softness of a woman, the unexpected gifts that life can surprise you with, without warning. How could I feel so good and hurt so much at the same time? Why did we ever have to let go?

With Mali's assurance that we would talk some more, and with my need to prepare for when we did talk, I left the Sand Bar. I left Mali behind.

A big mistake.

twenty-nine

....

I first noticed the green Olds just as I turned off Surf Road onto Grant Street. The second time was on Hollywood Boulevard. I glanced in the rearview mirror and there it was, riding in my wake.

Ten minutes later, southbound on the interstate, I still had my green shadow. If I was being followed, the driver was about as inconspicuous as the Mouseketeers riding Dumbo. There was one way to find out for sure. I turned off on the Ives Dairy Road exit ramp. So did the Olds. The light at the top of the overpass was red. I flipped on my left turn signal. So did the Olds. When the light changed, instead of turning, I rolled straight across Ives Dairy Road onto the entrance ramp for I-95. The green Olds was right behind me.

I was being followed. At least it wasn't a red Corvette. Whoever it was, was either an amateur or someone who didn't care if I knew I was being followed.

I continued south on I-95. There is no good way to get to Hialeah, which is why Florida's most stately thoroughbred racetrack is dying. The interstate is perpetually under construction. The Palmetto Expressway has a cruising speed of at-your-own-risk. City streets are peppered with traffic lights and four-way stop signs at almost every intersection. Between stops are school buses, garbage trucks crawling at the speed of a dying slug, cabs swerving recklessly around parked buses, confused tourists making abrupt U-turns, family vans dodging street vendors, and motorcycles maneuvering through it all. No matter which route I took it would be easy to lose the tail. But before I did, I wanted to know who was following me.

Traffic moved through the Golden Glades interchange like a constipated bowel movement. The green Olds was still tagging along. As cars finally dumped onto the Palmetto, demented motorists adjusted their blinders and broke from the pack for the maddening stretch drive.

I stayed on the expressway until the first exit, where I pulled off. After a hundred yards or so I slowed down and eased Loftus's Volvo off the asphalt onto the gravel shoulder. I parked the car. The green Olds pulled to a stop about twenty yards back. I cut off the ignition and waited. The Olds continued to idle. I got out of the car and started walking toward the green car. The Olds went into reverse and backed away. I stopped. I watched the driver shift into drive and speed past me. I had lost my tail, but not before I recognized the driver. I had been followed by the alleged beau of Eloise, the victim of Tigertail Bookkeeping, the one and only Ira Levy.

Levy would have the opportunity at a later date to explain why he was following me. Nick Triandos was waiting for me in the Promised Land. First things first. I had a job to do. I had to check out some naked dancers. It wasn't voyeurism. It was surveillance. There's a big difference. Elected officials, public servants, and morality's watchdogs surveil. All others are perverts and voyeurs and are going to go to hell because they enjoy life more than the always condemning self-righteous. Which is the real sin.

A holier-than-thou virus was spreading rapidly through Broward County municipalities. Cities were passing ordinances prohibiting the sale of alcoholic beverages in establishments featuring nude entertainment. The effect was the same as closing them down.

In Hallandale, an ever-vigilant city commissioner was quick to jump on the anti-skin wagon. The self-appointed guardian of the city's chastity proposed banning naked bars within the city limits. Problem was, Hallandale didn't have any nude bars. Not wanting to act blindly on all matters, the commissioner proposed that the entire city commission embark on an extended field trip to various girlie bars throughout Dade and Broward counties, just so they would know what it was they were banning.

• • •

In Hialeah, a twisting array of tricolored neon tubes brightly proclaimed:

THE PROMISED LAND
A FLESHTIVAL OF BEAUTY
ALL NUDE DANCERS
X X X

Adjacent to the building was a packed dirt lot with about a dozen cars. I didn't see Nick's Bronco. I parked between two chuckholes. No valet parking. No security guards. The neighborhood was too tough for rent-a-cops.

The dingy building appeared to have been colored with a mechanical pencil. There were iron grilles over the ink black windows. No free peeks at the paragons of femininity on parade.

I went inside. The air was dank and smelled of spilled booze, stale tobacco, and spent fantasies. The walls were covered with phony walnut panels patched with plywood. On the floor was a threadbare carpet the color of dried blood. The illumination came from beer signs and dim spotlights. A few cracked mirrors hung behind the bar. Ambiance by Vandals Interior-Design Studio.

A horseshoe-shaped three-foot-high stage covered about a fourth of the floor space. The stage's perimeter was rimmed with chairs. A bored-looking dancer with sagging water-balloon breasts was undulating in a trance onstage. A couple of young men were examining her, pondering careers in gynecology.

"Can I help you?" asked a husky female voice.

My eyes drifted from the dancer's goodies to the woman next to me. She was stocky and wore only a fringed bikini bottom. Her breasts shone like beacons of hedonism. Her eyes were dull.

I contemplated her breasts and said, "Do you work here?"

She glanced down at her bare chest and then up at me.

"What do you think?" she said in a genius-to-moron tone.

"Well, I thought maybe you were trying to make a good first impression."

She gave me a tired look. There are eight million come-on lines in the Naked City, and she had heard them all.

"You want a table?" she said.

"No, thanks. I'll sit at the bar."

The bar ran the length of one wall, with a runway stage behind it. It was currently occupied by a dancer in high-heeled boots, not a stitch more of clothing. She stopped in front of a guy sitting at the bar. He was wearing a suit. The dancer did a deep knee bend with her legs spread, giving the suit an unobstructed view of her promised land. The suit reached across the bar and stuffed a bill into the dancer's garter.

I looked for Nick, but didn't see him. I picked a stool at the end of the bar, strategically located so I could see both stages. A few more dreamers entered and sat ringside. I was approached by a buxom barmaid with streaked hair that looked like it had been shampooed and blown dry in a car wash. Her dress was plain, without ulterior motive.

Her lips curled into a nicotine-stained smile. "First time here?" she said.

I nodded.

"I thought so. I'd remember you."

"Aw, shucks," I said, "I bet you say that to all the boys."

She laughed. "As a matter of fact, I do. What'll it be?"

"The coldest beer in a bottle."

The music faded out. The dancer onstage lumbered off without fanfare or applause. The dancer behind the bar stood motionless, arms folded across her breasts, waiting for the next record. It was a loud, rhythmic beat. A dark haired girl of about eighteen sprinted onto the main stage and began gyrating to an annoyingly repetitious Latin tune. The dancer behind the bar must have been deaf. She moved like a zombie doing the stroll. By the end of the record the dancer onstage was also naked. I studied her thighs with academic interest. No blue owl tattoo. The prospect of sitting there waiting for Lola was beginning to depress me. Still no sign of Nick.

For almost an hour I waited for Nick and watched dancers in various sizes and shapes, anorexic to mammoth, take turns displaying their wares. An aging, peroxide mother, complete with stretch marks, shimmied about for five minutes. A bowling alley cutie shed everything but her illusion of stardom. She was followed by a motorcycle moll who eyed everyone contemptuously while slinking awkwardly through her routine. A pale beauty would bump and grind, then a dark vixen would hootchie-cootchie. At the end of the cycle, for the finale, all the dancers appeared for a clumsily staged chorus line au natural. Ripe and raw dancers aplenty. Then the rotation began again, as each dancer reappeared solo for her next set. Pounds of flesh but not one ounce of blue owl tattoo.

A dancer with full breasts and empty eyes stood on the edge of the bar and leaned over in front of me, swaying her qualifications inches from my face.

Enough was enough. I was worried about Nick. I had to find out what happened to him. The pay phone was in the men's room.

I called the Sand Bar, figuring Nick had either gone back there to work his shift or else he had left a message with Carla for me. I was wrong on both counts.

"I haven't heard from him," Carla said. "Is everything all right?"

"Yeah," I said. "We've probably just crossed paths. Listen, it looks like we may be tied up awhile. Can you cover the bar?"

"Of course."

"Thanks. I'll try to get Nick back there soon. If it gets too long for you, don't hesitate to close early if there's no business."

"Don't worry about the bar. I'll take care of it."

"I know you will."

"Harry? You and Nick take care."

"Not to worry," I said and hung up.

Nick must have left the Promised Land before I got there, and that was over an hour ago. It wouldn't have taken him that long to get back to the Sand Bar. That probably meant he'd spotted Lola after he called the Sand Bar. She had worked the day shift and when I didn't show up in time to relieve Nick, he must have followed her. There was no sense sitting in the Promised Land watching more women peel away their gift wrapping. Now I had to find Lola so I could find Nick.

I went back to the bar and asked the barmaid to total my tab.

I placed a twenty on the bar. "The change is yours if you can help me."

"Sorry, babe, I'm not that kind of girl."

"The story of my life," I said. "But that's not the kind of help I need. I'm looking for Lola."

"Who's Lola?" She was cool, didn't miss a beat or drop her poker face.

"The one with the blue owl tattoo."

She eyed me suspiciously. "I thought you haven't been here before."

"I haven't."

"Who are you?"

"A friend of Lola's."

"Well, friend of Lola's, take your change and leave. I don't sell that kind of information."

She was an experienced player, probably got a lot of requests for dancers' home numbers and addresses. It didn't matter. I knew how to beat her.

"Let me show you something."

"Don't unzip that thing in here. I've seen more than my share. You've seen one Eiffel Tower you've seen them all."

"You got a nasty mind," I said. "I like that." I took out my wallet and showed her the laminated copy of my private investigator's license. "Look, I appreciate the way you protect the dancers' privacy, but it's in Elsbeth's interest that I find her first."

Two things impressed her. That I knew Lola's real name and finding her "first."

"What do you mean 'first'?" She said her line as if I had written it for her.

"I'm also a bounty hunter," I said with a straight face. "It's not really Lola I want, but I have reason to believe the man I'm after is looking for her. If I can find Lola before he does I might be able to stop him."

It has to sound absurd enough not to be a lie.

She looked straight into my sincere eyes and broke up laughing. "Mister, that is the damnedest crock of shit I've heard in fifteen years in this business. Too bad it didn't work."

I gave her my dejected look. I wrote my name, address, and phone number on a bar napkin and showed her my picture driver's license to confirm the information.

"If I was out to harm Lola would I give you this?"

"No." She thought about it for a moment. "Listen, you want to see Lola, come back Monday. She'll be working the late shift."

"Monday it is," I said agreeably. It was time to play my hole card. "One last favor, though. Keep this," I said, pushing the napkin at her. "If a giant Greek comes in here looking for her, call me. He's about six six and roughly two hundred eighty pounds. He's got an olive complexion, short hair—"

"And a walrus mustache," she finished, suddenly believing me.

"He's been here?"

"This afternoon. Jesus Christ, mister, you're on the level."

"That's what I've been trying to tell you. Forget about Lola, it's the Greek I want. Do you know where he went?"

She shook her head. "No. He left without saying anything." Then it hit her. "My God! He left here right after Lola!"

She gave me Lola's address.

thirty

· · · · · · ·

The Crime Watch sign had been stolen. It was that kind of neighborhood. Three generations and cultures had taken their toll on what had originally been built as affordable family housing for World War II and Korean War veterans. War brides and hoola hoops had been replaced by post-Batista Cubans and plastic Madonnas on the dashboard, which in turn had been supplanted by Anglicized Latins and discount nesting possessions. French fries & gravy to black beans & rice to Whoppers & pizza.

Most of the houses, from fix-it-uppers to refugee shelters, had been neglected to varying degrees. It was not all single-family housing. Interspersed were duplexes and triplexes and a few family grocery stores. Many of the yards looked like Orange Bowl parking lots. A neighborhood beyond zoning violations.

It was getting dark, but still light enough for me to recognize Nick's Bronco parked next to a lavender Pontiac Firebird on the lawn of a triplex. The address matched the one for Lola that I had been given at the Promised Land. I parked the Volvo between the Firebird and a bottle-brush tree. I locked the doors. Lizards scrambled across the weed-infested sidewalk as I made my way around the parked vehicles.

Across the street an old couple in webbed lawn chairs watched me with casual interest. Ma and Pa Yucca, first-generation Cubans, who still took pride in keeping their home freshly painted and their yard landscaped.

The front of the triplex was hidden behind an un-manicured hedge. The yard was barren except for scattered clusters of sandspurs. Even though the day was fading into dusk, I could still make out the dark rust stains along the base of the wall, caused by the well-water sprinkler system, which had apparently dried up sometime ago. I had seen better homes and gardens.

Lola's apartment was at the far end of the building. I followed the narrow path between the overgrown hedge and the chipped concrete slab stoop. The evening news in Spanish and the smell of cooking arroz con pollo seeped from the first unit. The second apartment was dark, silent, and odorless.

The light was on behind the third door. I peered through the curtainless window. The room was cluttered with tape decks, microwaves, typewriters, personal computers, VCRs, TVs, piles of loose clothing, boxes, and stuffed plastic garbage bags. It looked as if someone had hit it big on *The Price Is Right*.

The front door was locked. I didn't see Nick or Lola inside, so I decided to try the back door.

As I rounded the corner, I tripped over two naked men lying in the dirt. They were alive and well and in the missionary position, bound together at the ankles, knees, waists, arms, and necks by duct tape. Their mouths were also taped shut. Performance art had finally made its way from New York to Miami. Or else Nick Triandos was nearby.

I stood up, picking sandspurs from my clothes. My

"assailants" were young Hispanics. I think even Sherlock Holmes would have fingered them as the two young movers that assisted Lola in cleaning out the Loftus apartment. They had pained expressions, from sandspurs or embarrassment.

One of them tried to mumble something through his taped lips.

"Sorry," I said. "I don't speak Spanish."

I turned and started for the back door. Realizing that I was going to leave them in human bondage, both men began making unintelligible noises with a distinct Cuban accent. I was sure I had been called worse.

The back door was open. The kitchen was filthier than the men's room in a Mississippi bus depot, and the stench was worse than a three-day-old open can of cat food. Empty bottles and dirty dishes were spewed about like leftovers from an unnatural act between consenting adults. The tile walls and the terrazzo floor were coated with a brown gook. I didn't look any closer.

Nick Triandos was sitting at the dinette set, his elbows resting on the tabletop. He was holding a blood-soaked compress to his forehead. It did not completely cover the gash above his eyebrow. I had missed the fight scene.

"You look like an outpatient who should have stayed in," I said.

"What kept you?" Nick said without looking up, as if he had been expecting me.

"I was having my heart removed," I said. "Now there's nothing left to break."

"What the hell are you mumbling about?"

"Nothing. Let me see."

Nick lifted the compress. The lump was bigger than the gash was deep.

"Lovely," I said. "The Siamese twins out back do that?"

He nodded. "They still there?"

"Dancing cheek to cheek, so to speak. Lola here?"

Nick gestured with his head. "In the bedroom."

"Don't get up. I'll find it."

"That must be why they call you the detective."

She was sitting on the bed with one leg tucked under her. The other leg was propped up, with her chin resting on the knee. Her toes were separated by torn tissue squares. She was painting her toenails. She wore lime-colored panties. That, and a blue owl tattoo on her inner thigh, was it. She saw me standing in the open doorway. She stared at me with cold, hard eyes. She didn't appear to be impressed with what she saw. But she was young.

"You Nick's friend?" She had a raspy voice.

"Yes."

"You got a name?" she said, concentrating once again on her toes.

"Harry," I said.

She nodded. "So, Dirty Harry, you going to beat me up and tie me up, or is that just Nick's thing?"

"Why don't you get dressed so we can talk."

She smirked. "If I'm embarrassing you, why don't you leave?"

"I need to talk to you first."

"So talk."

"It doesn't always have to be like this, Elsbeth," I said quietly.

The sound of her real name sent a slight shiver through her. For just a brief instant the hard facade of Lola cracked. I caught a glimpse of the lonely and profoundly hurting Elsbeth. Lola recovered quickly.

"The name is Lola." Her voice was bitter. "Got it?"

Seconds turned into moments. Finally I said, "All right. Have it your way. You remember Wade Loftus?"

"Christ, that jerk-off." She dipped the tiny brush into the bottle of polish. "What's his problem now?"

"You don't know?"

"Oh, I know. I can list his problems alphabetically. You want to hear them? A, he's an asshole. B, he's got a bird dick. C, he's crazy—"

"D, he's dead."

For all the reaction I got, I could have just told her the price of a professional pedicure.

"Yeah?" Do you need an appointment? "So what happened?"

"He was murdered," I said simply.

She shrugged, but kept her eyes on her toes. "Am I supposed to care?" Not a trace of emotion in her voice.

That stopped me. I kept my composure intact. "You tell me. He said he was in love with you. He hired me to find you. He wanted you to know that he was ready to marry you."

She ingested what I said and snickered.

"I'll be damned," she muttered, almost smugly. "What a fool." Then she returned to more important matters at hand—the little piggie that had roast beef needed more polish.

"I marvel at your compassion," I said with an edge to my voice.

"Do you?" She removed the tissue pieces between her wiggling digits. "Well, Dirty Harry, marvel at this."

Lola leaned back, legs stretched out, propped up on her elbows, so that her breasts jutted invitingly toward me. "You want compassion?" she said. "It'll cost you two hundred dollars."

"Is that the going rate?"

"No. That's a special rate just for you."

"I'm flattered."

"Don't be. Everybody else is free."

There was no denying that Lola had a body that could knock the wind out of a man's marriage. Her legs were porcelain smooth, her belly peach-fuzzed and flat, her breasts intoxicating. She was the total package. It was easy to understand how a man would be tempted, how Wade Loftus could play the fool for her. But it wasn't Lola I was staring at. I was thinking about Elsbeth, a hurt little girl, an emotionally wounded woman-child who never had the chance to be a kid. An abandoned daughter, forced to age from shy child to shameless woman with the death of her father. She had been left alone with no one to care for and no one to care for her. Her needs to protect and be protected were left unfulfilled. No one to hear her "Help me" or her silent prayers. So, as her body caught up to her forced-survival maturity, she discovered that when she exposed herself people noticed her and even conditionally cared about her. Men were suddenly interested in her. She attracted the masses of idiots who spelled "woman" p-u-s-s-y and the nitwits who valued boobs over brains. Maybe that was better than nothing, better than what she had. Elsbeth had been cheated of her youth. Sadly, not all forms of child molestation are fashionably illegal.

I felt for Elsbeth. I don't like to see people hurting.

And then there was Lola.

Nothing innocent about Lola. She had taken Wade Loftus for everything. It hadn't been enough to clean out the apartment. She was a greedy woman, who had to go back for Eloise's car and burglarize her office. But how did Lola know about the significant dates in Loftus family history? Why did she bother with the dates? Had she been trying to set someone up? Was she leaving messages?

I had to play the cards I was dealt. Two queens and a joker. Now the joker was dead. That left me with Lola and Eloise. Eloise and Elsbeth.

I tried looking beyond Lola, in search of Elsbeth. I looked at her full lips. I imagined her hair a different color. And that's when I finally saw it, right in front of me. I saw Elsbeth. I saw what Wade Loftus had been attracted to. Yes, she was young enough to be his daughter, but she was definitely his kind of woman.

"Get dressed," I said. "We're leaving."

Lola settled deeper into the bed. "Pity you couldn't stay longer."

I crossed the room to the nightstand and picked up the phone. Lola didn't move.

I dialed 911.

She sat up. "Who are you calling?"

"Yes. I want to report prowlers." I gave them Lola's address and Ira Levy's name. "How long? Thank you."

Suddenly vulnerable, Lola covered her breasts with her hands. "Who did you call?"

"You got five minutes before the police get here." I walked over to the door. "If you decide to leave with us, grab whatever you want to keep. You won't be coming back. The police will seize everything once they see what's here. Take anything that can identify you. I hope the lease isn't in your name."

"Bastard!" she spat. She hurled the bottle of nail polish at my head. I snatched it out of midair. No need to tell her it was a lucky catch.

"Four and a half minutes," I said.

I closed the door behind me. Something clanked on it from the other side.

Nick was in the kitchen, looking in the refrigerator.

I said, "You're a braver man than me, Gunga Nick."

"I'm looking for clues."

He was examining the expiration date on a jar of something gray.

"Let's go. The police are on the way."

"What about her?"

"If she's quick enough, she'll catch up to us."

We went out the back door.

Nick's naked attackers were still laid out like the main course at a gay banquet. They had rolled onto their side. Their eyes enlarged with a respectful fear when they saw Nick.

"Don't worry, fellows," I reassured them. "He won't be bothering you anymore. I've called the police. They're on their way over here to protect you."

They began to squirm, trying to free themselves from the tape.

As Nick stepped around them he said, "Hope you're practicing safe sex."

They mumbled something I couldn't understand. I really did need to learn a second language.

At the cars, Nick said, "Where to?"

"How's your head?"

"It's there."

"You need a doctor?"

"No."

"You want to go home?"

"Not particularly."

"You can always go back to the Sand Bar."

"Or?"

"Or you can follow me. I think I'm about to solve a murder."

Lola was cursing me as she came running around the hedge, still dressed in only the lime-colored panties. She was carrying a bundle tied in a sheet.

I opened the door to the Volvo. "Get in," I said.

"Bullshit," she hissed. "I'm not leaving my car."

She opened the trunk of the lavender Firebird. She threw the bundle in and untied it. She selected a garment or two.

I drove Lola's car while she dressed. What the hell. The Volvo was Loftus's. The police could trace it back to the law offices where Ira Levy worked.

It was a forty-minute drive to our destination. Nick was following us in his Bronco. Lola must have been shy around strangers. She didn't speak to me for the whole drive.

A little after eight o'clock we pulled into the parking lot.

Nick got out of his car and said, "Where are we?"

Lola had already started walking toward the building.

"I think I'm getting the silent treatment," I said.

Nick said, "She acts like she knows where she's going."

I nodded.

We followed Lola. She led us to the elevator, and inside she pushed the 4 button. On the fourth floor, still without coaxing or direction, Lola led us down the hall. She stopped in front of a door and pushed the doorbell.

Nick and I stood behind her and waited. The door opened.

Eloise Loftus was wearing a silk kimono. "Yes?" She looked at Lola and then at me and Nick. Then Lola. Eloise's eyes flashed, but the color drained from her face. Her lips moved twice without speaking before anything came out.

"Elsbeth?" she gasped.

With an almost sinister smile, Lola said coolly, "Hello, Mother."

thirty-one

•••••••••••••

It was not the mother and child reunion that balladeers sing about. Eloise and Elsbeth regarded each other with a strange fascination, as if they were studying their reflections in a time-warped mirror. Without a word Eloise recovered, her mask of control back in place. She stepped aside and let us in. She was not alone.

A curly-haired man wearing flannel slacks, a white shirt, suspenders, and a silk tie was leaning over the dining room table, shuffling through a sheaf of documents. Draped over a chair back was the matching jacket to his slacks. He glanced up and without acknowledging us went about his business.

Mundo Cruz sat on the couch, leafing through a magazine.

"Who's the old guy?" Nick said.

Cruz bristled. He dropped the magazine and stood up. The man at the table gave us his undivided attention. Eloise shook her head. Lola was a neutral observer.

I said, "Thanks for putting everyone at ease, Nick."

"What are you doing here?" Cruz said to me, his voice sounding as if it had marinated overnight in snake venom. I had the feeling he wasn't overly pleased to see me. "Who are these people?"

"We're here for the choir audition. Is there a sign-up sheet?"

A faint smile crossed Lola's lips. Cruz did not smile. He stepped around the couch.

The man at the table spoke. "I think introductions are in order. I'm Nathan Searle, one of Mr. Cruz's attorneys. I take it you know Mrs. Loftus and Mr. Cruz."

I nodded. "I'm Harry Rice. This is Nick Triandos."

"Cruz as in Mundo?" Nick said to me.

"The same."

Nick eyed Cruz and said, "Charmed, I'm sure."

"And that," I said, "leaves just the young lady. Eloise, do you want to introduce your daughter?"

Mundo Cruz blanched at my words. He walked over and studied Lola as if he were appraising an objet d'art. Then he turned and glared at Eloise. "This is Elsbeth? Look at her. She looks like a *puta*."

Quicker than a nightclub comic, Lola shot back, "Yeah, but you'll be dreaming about me next time you beat your meat, old man."

Cruz whirled and slapped her hard across the mouth with an open hand.

"Do not dare to speak to me like that again," he said evenly, without a twinge of apology, as if that was the way women were trained in the old country.

Holding her mouth, Lola peered at Cruz. "That'll be twenty bucks. It's another twenty if you want to hit me again, pervert." She said it calmly.

Cruz's body jerked. A guttural noise rumbled from his throat. His eyes twitched, crazed with outrage. He drew back a clenched fist and swung with the full thrust of his body at Lola's head.

Nick's massive hand shot up and wrapped around Cruz's fist inches before it smashed into the girl's temple.

"Try me," Nick said.

Cruz was startled. His face reddened. He tugged, but could not free his hand from Nick's grip.

"Let go, you sonofabitch," Cruz hissed.

Nick squeezed down harder on the fist.

Cruz flinched. His self-image had just been challenged by two unworthy opponents. An overgrown Greek bartender and peroxide vamp were treating the prestigious Mundo Cruz as if he was a common *Marielito*.

Nathan Searle's voice penetrated the mute room. "Perhaps we could all sit down and talk."

That eased the tension. Nick released his grip. Cruz slowly regained his color. He glared disgustedly at Lola, shaking his head. Then, as if something had just occurred to him, he turned to me.

"This," he said, "this is the go-go girl you were looking for?"

I nodded.

His whole body sagged as if the life had just gone out of it.

"I had no idea," he said.

• • •

We sat around the dining room table in an atmosphere of peculiar silence, as if we were preparing for a nocturnal seance to contact Wade's spirit. Of course, if my hunch was right, the only thing that would be materializing was Wade's murderer.

The impeccably groomed Nathan Searle, at one end, assumed the role of arbiter. An expressionless Cruz sat at the other end of the table. Eloise Loftus was across from me, motionless, staring disapprovingly at her daughter on my right. Nick settled for the comfort of the couch.

Nathan Searle opened. "Mr. Rice, suppose you begin by telling us why you are here."

"I just want to satisfy an obligation to a client," I said.

Eloise and Cruz both objected. Something about me being fired and paid off to get lost.

Searle held up a judicial hand. When the room was quiet, he said, "What client is that, Mr. Rice? It appears that your services have been terminated by all concerned."

"I wasn't working for the concerned," I said. "Wade Loftus was my client."

"That's nonsense," Eloise said.

"Is it?"

She glared contemptuously at me. "Wade detested you. He never would have hired you. Next thing we know you'll be telling us that Elsbeth hired you, too."

"No," I said. "Actually, Wade hired me to find Elsbeth. Ironically, as it turns out, by hiring me to find her, he unwittingly hired me to find the solution to his own murder."

Puzzlement flickered across Eloise's face. "What are you saying? Elsbeth killed Wade?"

Lola spoke up. "Right." She gave me a scornful look. Another lost vote for Mr. Congeniality. "What did I do, fuck him to death?"

I said, "Well, in a manner of speaking."

"No way, asshole. I never killed anyone."

The foul-mouthed Lolita had Mundo Cruz shaking his head with an odd shame. "What's going on, Rice?" His tone was almost neutral. No trace of anger or any emotion.

I had tested the water long enough. It was time to take the plunge.

I looked at Lola. "It's your story. You want to tell it?"

Lola held up a finger.

I shrugged. "Stop me if I get it wrong," I said to her, though it was intended for everyone.

thirty-two

• • • • • • • • • • • • •

"*It wasn't until a little* while ago that everything fell into place," I began. "Well, not everything. There are still a few 'why's' I don't have the answers to. But to paraphrase the Cheshire cat, it doesn't matter how you walk, as long as you get there. And to get there we need to begin several months ago when a young dancer named Lola visited the law office of Wade Loftus.

"According to Wade, Lola approached him to represent her. He specialized in entertainment and sports law. She was an entertainer. Only when Lola asked Wade to be her agent, he doesn't say yes right away, but he doesn't forget her. Then one night, in the throes of loneliness, having just seen his beloved wife off on a train, Wade stops by Fort Bush to check out his prospective client's talents. A little business to take his mind off his personal blues. One thing leads to another, and Wade invites Lola home to play house with him while his wife is away. Of course, poor unsuspecting Wade had no idea that he was playing with his wife's daughter."

I faced Lola. "But you knew. You knew exactly who Wade Loftus was and who he was married to."

Lola's eyes narrowed, but she didn't say a word.

Mundo Cruz said, "That's disgusting. It makes no sense. Why would she knowingly hustle her own mother's husband? She couldn't have known."

"Of course she knew," Eloise said.

Cruz's brow furled as he struggled with that notion. "I don't understand. Why would she want to seduce your husband?"

"To get even, you old fool," Eloise snapped. "She was trying to get back at me because I divorced Latham. Because I chose not to live my life married to a bottle. Because she's a conniving little tramp who's the product of Latham's upbringing. She has no one to blame but herself. It was her decision. She's the one who wanted to live with Latham. She chose him over me. Let's not have any misdirected sympathies here. Let's not forget how she waited until her birthday to help herself to all my household belongings. Her little joke on Mommy. She waited until my anniversary to steal my car. Oh, she was having all kinds of fun at Mommy's expense. She waits until Wade's birthday to break into my office. Does that satisfy her perverse sense of fun? No. What does? Killing my husband?"

"No." Lola's lips barely move. "No," she murmured again, sounding like a faraway echo. She looked up at everyone around the table except her mother. Some of the hardness of Lola had begun to dissipate as the softness of Elsbeth began to surface. "It's not true. I didn't steal her car. I never broke into her office. I couldn't kill anyone."

I reached over and took her hand in mine. She sighed heavily and squeezed my hand before she pulled away.

Nathan Searle said, "Elsbeth."

She looked at him.

He said, "Did Wade Loftus know who you were? Did he know you were his wife's daughter?"

"No," she said.

"You never told him?"

"No." Then after a moment of reflection, she said, "I was going to tell him. I wanted him to know. I wanted her to know. I was just waiting for the right time. Then, I don't know, I just thought, she's not worth it."

Searle leaned forward. "Why did you do it? Is it the reason your mother said?"

"That was part of it."

"What other reasons did you have?"

"Ask her."

"No, Elsbeth. This is your little drama," Eloise said dispassionately. "You play your little scene without me."

"Without you," Elsbeth repeated, her voice flat. She nodded. "Why should this be any different? When were you ever there? You didn't even respond to Daddy's death notice I sent you. You never asked if I needed anything, help with school or finances. I've done everything else without you. What right do I have to a mother? I grew up without you. I watched my father drink himself to death without you. Because of you."

"Latham was a drunk," Eloise said. "Don't blame me for that. I didn't do that to him."

"It's not what you did to *him*. It's what you did to *me*!" Elsbeth cried, the pain so apparent in her young eyes. "All that time you thought you were hurting Daddy, but you were tearing me apart. Why couldn't you leave us alone? You had everything. You wanted the car and the house and the furniture. You got it all. Daddy didn't care. All he wanted was me. You didn't even help with child support.

"But we didn't need your precious money. Daddy and I had each other. We didn't need anything else. Our little house was enough for us. But you wouldn't leave us alone. Every time Daddy was able to save a little money, you would take him back to court for child custody. You never wanted me. You just used me as an excuse so Daddy would have to spend his money on lawyers. As soon as we were broke again, you'd no longer contest my custody. You never wanted me.

"Remember what you'd say to me when you used to call? You'd tell me that Daddy stole me from you. You said that Daddy was an asshole. You said he was stupid. You told everyone, all your friends, all our friends, that he was no good. You were so concerned about getting your friends' sympathy, you didn't see how it was affecting me. And those few times I visited you on holidays, do you remember what you would tell me? You'd say that whenever I wasn't home Daddy would bring strange women into our house and have sex with them. Do you remember that? I was twelve years old and you were telling me that my father was fucking strange women! You were so full of hate. What did you want from me?"

"Very touching, Elsbeth," Eloise said. "Do you want to trade hard-luck stories? My parents died. I didn't leave them. They left me. I didn't leave you. You're the one who wanted to live with Latham. You left me. You ran away from me."

"I was not a runaway!" Elsbeth cried. "I was a throwaway!"

We were all momentarily silent, shaken by her anguish.

Mundo Cruz said, "My God, Eloise, what have you done to her?"

"Don't you see what she's doing?" Eloise said defensively. "Don't be fooled by those tears. She's just trying to make us forget."

"Forget what?" I said.

"That . . . that . . ." Eloise groped for a second. "That she stole my car. That she broke into my office."

I said, "Elsbeth didn't do that."

"Of course she did. She had to. No one else could have. She had copies of my keys made. You told me that. Who else knew that it was my anniversary and Wade's birthday? Who else could it have been?"

"Wade," I said.

"That's preposterous."

"Not if you think about it. Wade had the means, opportunity, and motive. You know he was planning to divorce you. He had already started liquidating your joint holdings. He was selling off the gun collection without your knowledge. Let me ask you something. Did you report your stolen car to the police?"

"Yes. Of course."

"You did?"

"Well, not me. Wade called them."

"Were you there when he called?"

"No."

"I don't think he reported it. Wade knew your routine. He knew you'd be at the health spa. I believe Wade took your car and sold it, because afterward you didn't replace it with a new one. Wade leased one for you, which he charged to the law office's accounts. As far as your office goes, Wade was on campus that night, teaching a class. It was a simple matter to go to your office after class and let himself in. If he's seen, who is going to question your husband for picking up a few things that you forgot?"

"But why?"

"To divert your attention from his selling off your things. Waiting until your anniversary to steal your car may have been his way of toying with you once he learned that your apartment had been burglarized on your daughter's birthday. It was a natural for him to hit your office on his birthday. He had to do something. He became concerned that you would find out that he had been selling the guns. He wanted to give you something else to think about. That's why I misunderstood Mundo's involvement. Until now."

Cruz glared at me. "Be careful, Rice," he warned.

"You could have saved your money, Mundo, if you had just been patient. By the time you paid me off, I had already learned that Loftus had been selling the gun collection. I was ready to quit before you intervened. I have to admit, your interest did confuse me.

"Still, that probably would have been the end of our association if Wade hadn't been murdered. That changed everything. I was questioned by the police, naturally enough, all things considered. During the police interview I'm told that Wade was involved with gun smuggling. It seemed that whenever Wade's name was mentioned, it was always connected to guns. Makes me think that guns are somehow responsible for his demise. And once again, Mundo, you send Carmen to see me. You want to know if I said anything to the police about you. All right, I understand that. You're a paranoid egotist. The whole world has nothing better to do than talk about Mundo Cruz. Of course, that was when I began to wonder if gun smuggling was your connection with Wade Loftus. I started thinking that was why you paid me off to quit investigating Wade. You knew if I looked long enough it would lead me to his gun-smuggling activities that would lead me to you.

"At least that's what I thought then. But then I find out from Eloise that you are her godfather. She also tells me that she told you about the gun collection being stolen. Being a concerned *padrino*, I imagine you put out the word that you were interested in the collection. Easy enough for a man with your . . . your what? Connections? Influence? Nice respectable words.

"And what does Mundo discover? He finds out the gun collection was being sold before it was reported stolen. Which is why you sent Carmen to scare me away once you found out Eloise had hired me. You knew what I was going to find out. When Carmen's knife trick didn't work, you bought me off. But by then it was too late. I already knew what Wade was up to. Now, as I look back, I realize you didn't want me out of the picture to protect yourself. You were trying to protect your god-daughter.

"So what exactly was it you didn't want Eloise to know? Did you find out something else about Wade that you didn't want me to discover? Something like he was going to dump his wife for a little bimbette? Or was Wade going to try and bilk Eloise out of her share of their joint holdings? What was it, Mundo? Something you wanted to protect Eloise from to such an extent that you would run me off. Is there any limit to what you would do to protect her? Would you do anything for her? Would you kill for her?"

Nathan Searle said, "Let me caution you, Mr. Rice—"

Mundo Cruz interrupted him, "Be still, Nathan." Cruz sat as stiffly, and almost as lifelike, as a statue in Madame Tussaud's Wax Museum. His stare was uncompromising. "What else do you think you know, Rice?"

Eloise looked up. "What?" Her eyes darted from Cruz to me. "Mundo killed Wade? Mundo killed Wade," she said again slowly, as if trying it on for size.

A tremor rippled across Cruz's stony countenance.

"Now what do you think of her, Mundo?" I said. "What do you think of a woman who would accuse her own daughter and her godfather of a murder that she committed?"

Cruz shook his head in disgust. "Hell is too good for her," he pronounced.

It took a moment to register before Eloise understood that I had just accused her of the murder of her husband.

"This is getting absurd!" she snapped. "First he accuses Elsbeth, then Mundo, and now me. I think he's covering for himself. Wade's body was found in his car."

"I never accused Elsbeth," I corrected. "I simply said Elsbeth was the solution."

"*You* accused me, Eloise," Cruz said.

"Don't be stupid," she chided. "You know what I meant."

"Yes. I know what you meant."

Eloise pressed her fingers against her forehead. "I was out of town."

"There are a couple of holes in your alibi," I said. "Two things in particular gave you away. A flat tire and a call to an unlisted phone number. I should have picked up on that this morning, when you called me at home. I never gave you my number. You must have taken it the day we went to Sara's for drinks. Afterward, we went to my house and you asked to use my phone. That's when you took my number."

"So what? What does that prove?"

"Wade didn't have my home number. That's why he showed up on a Sunday morning at the Sand Bar to see me. As it turns out, the last number dialed on Wade's office phone was my home number. Wade didn't have it. So who did?"

"There are a number of ways someone can get an unlisted number," Searle pointed out.

"I'm aware of that. What first aroused my suspicions was when Eloise insisted on giving me information I didn't need. Eloise, you went out of your way to see me, just to tell me where you were when Wade was murdered. I couldn't help but wonder why."

"Some people are just nervous talkers." Searle sounded like he was test driving the defense.

"I understand that. Without a motive, I wouldn't even

have considered it. She's not going to kill Wade because he wants a divorce. I found the motive when I found Elsbeth. It took a while for me to see the family resemblance, but I was sure of it when Eloise opened the door and saw her daughter. There was my motive. Wade Loftus was killed because he had the hots for his wife's daughter."

Searle said, "The lady says she was out of town."

"The police even have a witness who saw Wade leave here a half hour before Eloise did," I acknowledged. "I'll even bet there's a motel upstate that has proof Eloise spent the night there. But in between leaving here and checking into a motel, Eloise ran into the unexpected. Her husband still in the parking lot changing a flat tire. If it hadn't been for that flat tire, Wade Loftus would probably still be alive. Detective Stranahan called it to my attention when he said I wasn't much of a detective because I couldn't see the significance of a flat tire. The flat tire defined the crime. It was a crime of passion.

"I don't believe Eloise planned to kill him. According to her, that Sunday she and Wade got into a heated argument. Somehow during the course of that argument I think Eloise realized that his illicit affair was with her daughter. How many Elsbeths are there? That had to be devastating. Her husband and her daughter. Maybe not incestuous, but just as shocking to her. Eloise confronts Wade with this. I'm sure it caught him by surprise as well. Even Wade was bright enough to realize the ramifications. It wouldn't make for favorable press. Wade needed time to think. He hadn't planned this. So he walked out. He didn't know what else to do. He had to buy time.

"Left alone, Eloise stews for about half an hour and decides she's had enough. She is not going to wait around any longer. She packs a bag and leaves. In the parking lot she's surprised to find Wade still there, changing a tire. I figure the argument was reignited and in the heat of the moment, Eloise stabbed him. It's a simple matter to push the body into the open trunk and drive the car to the law offices. There she calls a taxi. Knowing the phone is equipped with last-call memory, she has to erase the number for the cab company so the police can't trace her. She punches in my number. Makes me the fall guy. After all, the body is in my car."

Eloise didn't say a word. She hadn't moved. She could have been a still-life on canvas. I couldn't even see her breathing.

Searle spoke. "What about a weapon? Or do you hypothesize that Mrs. Loftus routinely packs a stiletto in her purse?"

"No, she probably doesn't," I conceded.

"Then with what did she allegedly stab him?"

"A screwdriver." It was Eloise who answered without emotion. She turned to her daughter. "Are you happy now, Elsbeth? Are we even?"

Elsbeth's eyes were tearing. "You were always so proper. My mother, the college professor," she said, her voice racked with pain. It was all Elsbeth, Lola was gone. "I tried so hard to be everything that you're not. I didn't want to be anything like you. I bleached my hair. I got a tattoo. I took my clothes off in public." She stopped and swallowed. In the midst of her crying, she smiled. "It's so sad, it's almost funny. As hard as I tried not to, I succeeded in being exactly like you, only without the fancy facade."

Mundo Cruz examined Eloise with a cold detachment. With an icy voice he said, "What kind of mother are you, Eloise? What have you done to your daughter?"

"Don't you dare get self-righteous with me!" Eloise shot back. "Where were you all those years? You think checks raise children?"

"Be still, Eloise," Cruz ordered.

"She's the product of your desertion," Eloise continued. "You had to save face. Couldn't soil your precious reputation or your sainted family's name."

"Shut up!" Cruz was on his feet.

"Catholics can't get divorced. Such a holy man, Mundo." Eloise started laughing. She turned to Elsbeth. "I've got news for you, sweetie."

"No!" Cruz shouted.

"Not only are you exactly like your mother, you're just like your father. Say hello to your daddy."

Cruz slumped into his chair. He looked incredulously at Eloise. "You had to do that?"

"No, I didn't have to," she said coolly. "I just wanted you to share in our daughter's plight. I think it's time we did more as a family."

Cruz inhaled deeply and let it out slowly. He turned to Searle and said wearily, "Nathan, call the police."

Nathan Searle nodded and went to make the call.

Elsbeth hardly reacted, she just stared into oblivion refusing to acknowledge what she had just heard. Slowly her head started shaking in denial.

I took out my wallet and found that I still had Dr. Espineta's business card. I slid the card over to Elsbeth.

"Call her," I said. "She's good. She can help you. She saw me through some rough times."

Elsbeth pushed my hand away, but she kept the card.

I glanced at Nick and motioned toward the door. Our work was done. The posse was on its way. It was time for the Lone Ranger and his faithful Greek companion to ride off into the traffic.

epilogue

· · · · · · · · · · · ·

Alden Wooley's story made the front page. I was vindicated only to the extent that the murderer was identified. The article did suggest that I might have provided a dab of assistance to Alden during his investigation.

Nick Triandos paid a visit to the law offices for me. Ira Levy willingly told Nick that he was only following me to find out where I lived, so he could retrieve the leased Volvo the law offices were paying for.

Wade Loftus is still dead.

Eloise is awaiting trial.

I don't know what's become of Elsbeth or if Lola still exists.

· · ·

"His Dolly Parton wig encouraged a smile. It looked as natural as Thelonious Monk at the piano. He leaned closer to the mirror and plucked a stray hair from above his nose. From the city of bottles on the dresser, he selected a container of blue eye shadow. It would help, but there really wasn't much one could do with eyes that looked like an overcast sky. One last drag on the Chester-field and he would do his nails. Lt. Doster McGlamory was about to go undercover."

Stacey Shore opened her used bookstore on the Board-walk. About twice a week she comes into the Sand Bar to recite her latest chapter in progress.

"Marketing, that's why church attendance is down. Look at the Baptist. Every Baptist church is the first Bap-tist church. First Baptist Church of this street. First Bap-tist Church of Florida. First Baptist Church of the World. If it's the first Baptist church, that implies there's going to be more. So if I'm a sinner driving by, I say, 'Well, there's the first one. I'll stop at the third or fourth one. I got time.' What the Baptists ought to do is rename their churches. Call them the Last Baptist Church of whatever. Then if I'm a sinner driving by, I'm gonna think, 'Whoa! The last one! I better stop and get saved before it's too late.' Make them think it's the last stop before damna-tion."

Father Shifty continues to conduct regular services at the Sand Bar. His message is the same: God is better than the one packaged in churches and sold on television.

I like to believe that Father Shifty is right.

• • •

A few weeks went by without hearing from Mali. In all my blundering, I had not gotten her new phone number or address. I didn't know Phillip's last name. I tried to call her at the college, only to be told that she was on sabbat-ical. A couple days after that, my friend Cat called me. She told me she had heard from Mali.

"How is she?" I asked.

"She's fine. She asked me to call you."

"Why doesn't she call me?"

"She can't."

"She can't? Why?"

Cat hesitated. "She's afraid it would bother Phillip."

"So what? Let it bother him. It's not like he owns her. This is incredible. Mali can't have friends because insecure little Phillip doesn't trust her. Who the hell does he think he is?"

"Her husband, Harry. Mali and Phillip are married."

It's been two months now since I last saw Mali and she said we'd talk some more. We haven't. And I don't know why. I think I hope that the three of them—Phillip, Phillip's wife, and Chuckie's shadow—are more content than I am. I know that the Mali I once knew is no more. That beautiful free spirit had been captured and tamed, her soul imprisoned. It makes no sense.

I don't know. Maybe I had been chasing an illusion.

☗ HarperPaperbacks *Mysteries by Mail*

The Weaver's Tale by Kate Sedley

It is the 15th century. A man has been murdered, and the brother of a respected citizen hanged for the crime. Months later, the victim turns up alive—only to be murdered a second time. Who is the killer and how might this all be connected to a nobleman's fancy?

Drift Away by Kerry Tucker

Photojournalist Libby Kincaid learns that her friend Andrea has been murdered by the accused killer she had been defending. Libby goes undercover at Andrea's cutthroat law firm and finds herself in the hot seat as she comes close to a murderer.

Homemade Sin by Kathy Hogan Trocheck

When feisty Callahan Garrity of House Mouse Cleaning Service hears of her cousin's murder, she dons a detective cap and does a job on grease and crime in Atlanta.

Parrot Blues by Judith Van Gieson

A chief suspect in the kidnapping of Neil Hamel's client and her rare macaw has expired. To find out more, Neil enters a dangerous game of bird-smuggling and one-upmanship. So far, the only eyewitnesses are parrots—and they're not talking.

The Trouble with Thin Ice
by Camilla T. Crespi

A bride-to-be, is arrested for a very cold-blooded murder—the week of her wedding. Simona Griffo, a friend who likes to meddle in such matters, starts asking questions. As she puts the pieces together, however, she unwittingly pushes herself onto thin ice.

Hearing Faces by Dotty Sohl

Janet Campbell's neighbor has been brutally killed, and there's no apparent motive in sight. Yet Janet refuses to live in fear. When a second murder strikes the apartment complex , Janet's life turns upside-down. Seeking answers she discovers greedy alliances, deadly secrets, and a vicious killer much too close to home.